I0653018

# My Forever

### By J. B. Mericle

© 2013 J. B. Mericle
ISBN: 978-0-615-93168-5
Cover by G.S.
Editor: Rachel R.

# ACKNOWLEDGMENTS

First, I want to thank my good friend Rachel for motivating me to write. Without our daily texts and you telling me I have the sporadic thoughts for writing, this never would have happened. Not to mention your fabulous editing skills.

Secondly, I want to thank my husband Dustin. If not for you telling me that I was reading too much and needed to find a new hobby, I wouldn't be here. Most importantly thank you for implying that I couldn't write, so that I would want to prove you wrong.

Third, I want to thank my brother Sam. Without you telling me that I should get back into writing, I don't think I ever would have accepted my husband`s dare.

None of this could've happened without you guys. Thank you so much.

# Table of Contents

# Chapter 1

## *How I got here*

Have you ever had one of those moments where you wonder how in the hell did I get here? Well, I am having one of those moments right now. Where's here you ask? I'd like to call it my own personal hell. Okay, so not literally hell. But still, it is hot and I'm on the side of the road having a panic attack. Why you ask? I`m about to see my first love. Can you really say first love if the other person didn't know you were in love with him? Oh well, that's what we're calling him. His name is Jackson Calright, or Jax for short. God he`s handsome, rich brown hair that you just want to run your hands thru and piercing blue eyes. I have thought about running my hands through his hair on more occasions than I care to admit.

I guess I should introduce myself. My name is Emily, Emily Day to be exact. I am an only child. My parents died in a car accident when I was twenty, so that just leaves my grandmother, Christine, as far as blood family goes. I`m twenty-six now and I work as a nurse at the local hospital. I`m pretty normal and boring, to say the least. I have long, strawberry blonde hair, blue eyes and more freckles than I can count. My grandmother calls them `beauty marks`. Personally, I wish they would all join together and give me the perfect tan. I`m not fat, but it probably wouldn't hurt to lose a few pounds. I have always been curvy, sporting an hour glass figure. I think my size is short and cute, being five feet-two inches and weighing in at one hundred twenty-five pounds. My big boobs and butt being my highlighted features, of course. I`ve dated and had relationships in the past, I just haven't been able to find Mr. Right.

I met Jackson when I was fifteen. It was just any normal day at church on Sunday morning until he walked in. He was wearing faded blue jeans that hugged his thighs and a buttoned up flannel shirt that he had tucked in. I never was one to like flannel until I saw it on his body. I remember thinking yum! Inappropriate for church I know, but he had that aura about him that you just couldn't resist staring at, especially the way he walked, confidence rolled off of him in waves. He even rode a motorcycle. A black sports bike to be exact. It was HOT! He didn't look my way once that day. God! That was insulting.

I worked at throwing myself at Jackson for two years. It never worked; all he saw me for was a close friend who he hung out with. I remember when I was seventeen, I gave it one final attempt. No guts, no glory, right? We were at a football game and my friend Annabelle convinced me it was time to tell him how I felt. What's the worst that could happen, right? (Boy, I wish I could take that day back). Any who, I don't remember how, but I got him to come to my old beat up red Mitsubishi car. I was sitting in the driver's seat and he was in the passenger seat. I remember thinking, I can do this! I explained to him that I had a crush on him and wanted to be more than friends. (Okay if I was being honest it was more like head over heels in love, but I couldn't tell him that or he would've run away.) I remember the moment of total humiliation when he turned away from me, looking out the front window, saying, "I'm too old for you." With that, he got up and exited the car. I was seventeen and he was twenty. That's not that old. Yes, it might be considered illegal in some states, but my parents couldn't have cared less. I left the parking lot as quickly as I could and cried all the way home. This was before cell phones were popular, meaning I had to wait to call my best friend until I got home. I had tried and failed miserably to scheme my way into his pants for two years. When I laid it all out there for him, he wouldn't even look me in the eye to turn me down. It was like I wasn't good enough for him. Maybe I wasn't pretty enough, too fat, I don't know. But to this day, I still wonder what it was that made him turn me down so easily. It couldn't have been just about my age. I avoided him after that. I just didn't have the courage to face him again.

So why I am forcing myself into seeing the man who broke my heart all those years ago, you ask? It's because he will be at my best friend Annabelle's wedding this weekend. With all of the bridal party being out of town guests, she decided to make it an all-inclusive affair. Having the bridal shower, bachelor parties, family meet and greet, rehearsal and wedding all in a few days. Four days to be exact. Four days of complete agony if you ask me. I'm not one to not like weddings, I just don't like the ones where Jackson is going to be present.

I met Annabelle when I was thirteen at church, as well. We were stuck to each other like glue. She has that natural beauty where she never needs makeup. With her long brown hair, hazel eyes, a perfect figure and a super sweet personality. I swear she couldn't be mean, even if she tried. If she wasn't my best friend, I would've hated her guts.

This brings me to now. Here I am sitting in my car freaking out! I haven't seen him in almost ten years. Dropping my head back against the headrest, I let out a sigh. *UGH!* Trying to calm my nerves, I take several deep breaths, but it`s not working. I couldn't even attempt to drive if I wanted to, seeing how my palms were so sweaty my hands would slip right off the steering wheel. I hear pep talks work. "Right!" I respond out loud. *Great, now I'm talking to myself!*

Exasperated, I sit in silence trying to rein in my nerves before I get back on the road. After a few minutes have passed, I look out the window. It's a beautiful day with the sun starting to set over the horizon. Nothing surrounds me except fields of grass and pretty purple flowers. It's quite peaceful, if you ignore the cars going down the road to my left. I decide to make the best of it; no more pushing off the inevitable. I have to face the music. With that said, I put the car into gear and slowly make my way back onto the road.

I try to ignore the thoughts flooding my mind about what I will run into when I get there. Will he be there already? Will he recognize me? Hell, will he even remember me? I keep driving the last few miles down the narrow road toward my destination. I know I'm almost there. I have been driving close to twelve hours already. In attempts to drown out my current thoughts, I roll down the windows and turn up the radio. Everyone knows music can set your mood, and I'll try anything at this point. It just so happens, "Free Falling" by Tom Petty comes on the radio. I LOVE this song. Who honestly can't sing along to this song? I'm singing my heart out when the Garmin interrupts, advising me to take a right in half a mile. It's like hitting the kill switch. I feel the dread start to creep in the closer I get to the turn. Following my Garmin, I take a deep breath and make a right onto the gravel road called Hendricks Lane.

It all seems so surreal. Beautiful big oak trees line the driveway and moss is hanging off several trees up in the distance. When I see a house up the road, I turn off the GPS. I continue driving until I see cars parked on the left side of the house. Pulling into an open spot, I park my blue Jetta next to a red Toyota pickup truck and a white Ford Fusion. Taking a long look out the car window, I admire all the beauty that surrounds me. There is an old traditional white country farmhouse with a beautiful wrap-around porch to my right. A decent sized red barn is directly in front of me a couple yards away. The house is surrounded by fields of flowers and beyond that are trees. It's completely breathtaking; I can see why Annabelle would want to get married here. Crap, I don't even have a guy in my life and I can see myself getting married here.

Knowing it is getting late and starting to get dark outside, I muster up all of the courage I can. Closing my eyes, I repeat to myself, *I can do this*! I open my eyes and take one last look in the rear view mirror. *God!* I should've pulled over and freshened up. I'm wearing a plain white tank top that crisscrosses in the back and a blue and white striped maxi skirt. Thinking back, I should've put on something a little more flattering. Oh well. Frantically running my fingers through my hair to tame the madness, I reach in my pocket to grab my lip gloss. Turning off the car, I take a deep breath before applying gloss to my lips. Grabbing my purse, I open up the car door while chanting to myself, *I can do this! I can do this*! It's only four days. Anyone can survive four days. Lifting my legs out of the car, I step out and onto the grass. *Ugh*. Flip flops mixed with gravel and grass. *Great!* Watch me fall and bust my ass. Shutting the car door behind me, I pop my neck and roll my shoulders, trying to ease the tension from my body. I have got to pull my life together. Standing up tall, I square my shoulders. I will go in there with my head held high. *I can do this*! Not to mention it's getting late and I still need to get settled. With my luck, he's probably staring out the window right now, laughing at me. With that thought,

I set off towards the front door of the house.

## Chapter 2

*Does he even remember me?*

The walk up to the wooden front steps seems to take forever. Granted it is only about thirty steps, I linger on each step, still prepping myself and trying not to trip; I am known as the proverbial klutz. *For the love of god, get it together!* I am a twenty-six year old professional woman. He is just a man and I am no longer an innocent virgin. I have grown up; I am not that hormone induced teenager anymore. I`ve got this!

There aren't even that many cars outside, he probably isn't even here. I can just go in and say hi quickly, find out which room I am staying in, unpack and hit the sack. One night avoided. That sounds like a reasonable plan. Yep, that's what I`m going to do. With another sigh, I find myself right smack in front of the porch. Forging ahead, I take the steps ringing the doorbell.

Annabelle`s fiancé, Conner, answers the door. He is a strapping man with his tall slender body and blonde hair. But, what makes him alright in my book, is that he absolutely adores her.

"Hi Conner," I say quickly.

"Hi Emily, so glad to see you. Come on in. I will get Annabelle," he says before turning around and shouting, "ANNABELLE!"

Walking into the foyer, I see Annabelle bouncing from the back. "Emily, Oh my goodness! You`re here! YAY!" Annabelle squeals, stopping in front of me to give me a big hug. "Everyone is in the back," she says cautiously.

"Everyone..." I say nervously, watching Conner walk to the back of the house.

"Yes, he got here about an hour ago. I doubt he will even remember that day sweetie. Just act like it never happened," she assures me, "now come on, let's get you a drink and mingle."

"Honestly Annabelle, if you could just show me to my room, I'd love to get settled and go right to sleep. I`m really tired." Just go for it please, I don't want to see him. Not yet, at least let me primp for a bit. You know, shower, shave, and maybe have liposuction. If only she could read minds, that would be fabulous.

"No can do Em, I`m not having you avoid him and make my wedding week miserable. I had no idea Conner was going to put him as a groomsman."

This is true. Annabelle found out and tried to talk Conner out of it for at least a month. He assured her that Jackson has never mentioned us having an issue. Actually, my name was never brought up at all. I guess it helped that I lived far away from them. She was right though; I needed to suck it up.

"Okay, but you better make that drink is a strong one!" I suggest.

"YAY! I knew you would see it my way girl. This weekend is going to be so much fun," she replies excitedly.

Walking arm and arm, we head down the hallway toward the back. I notice the living room to the right followed by a formal dining room, and an old oak staircase to the left. We keep going straight ahead until we land in the kitchen. At first glimpse, I notice the kitchen is huge. There are white cabinets topped with black countertops, complete with an island in the middle. Man, I love this house with its old charm and updated renovations. Looking around, I see the dining room table is situated in front of a big bay window at the back of the kitchen and that's where I see him. *God! Did he get cuter? Sweet mercy! How's that even possible?* Prying my eyes to look anywhere but at Jackson, I see Brooke and Nathan Mitchell are here. They are friends of Annabelle's that I have met in the past. Continuing around, I notice Conner has resumed his seat at the table.

Annabelle announces to everyone, "Look who finally made it! Emily, everyone. Everyone, Emily," she says waving her hand back and forth between me and the table of people, "Now the whole wedding party is here!"

Everyone turns and looks at me, almost simultaneously. *God!* It's one of those moments, where if you didn't know someone had just acknowledged you, you would've sworn that you had toilet paper stuck to your foot. Standing stark still, I lift my hand and wave hesitantly while mumbling, "Hi." Sneaking a peak at Jackson, I find him staring at me. I`m pretty sure I turned as red as a fire truck, since I could actually feel the blood rushing to my face. Trying not to give anything else away, I turn my eyes quickly to Annabelle, who is currently shouting at me.

"Emily! Here is your margarita. Brooke and I made them, and let me tell you, they are delicious."

"Thanks," I reply. Taking my glass, I take a hefty sip and watch Annabelle walk to the table.

"Come on over here and join us Emily," Conner says grabbing a chair from the formal dining room and pulling it up to the table, "Were playing poker."

Taking another big gulp of my drink, I make my way over to the table and sit down next to Annabelle. Damn, these things are good. They are strong, but just what I need. On a good note, my chair is on the other side of the table from Jackson. Bad news, this means every time I look up, I look directly at him! *UGH!* Letting them finish their round of poker, I sit back and listen to them discussing the barn and plans for it tomorrow. Since I'm not familiar with the place, I just relax in my seat while I work on finishing off my drink.

Noticing my glass is almost empty, Brooke gets up and brings the pitcher of margaritas to the table. Now I remember why I like her! She likes to drink like me. *My kind of girl*! After about my third glass, I'm feeling good. I try all night not to peak over the rim of my glass too much at Jackson. Every time I do, I squirm in my chair. He has gotten even more delicious with his brown hair, piercing blue eyes, chiseled jaw, not to mention that smile, and his well-defined arms. Just imagining what his chest looks like or how it would feel, makes me all hot and bothered. *Geez!* I need to stop drinking. At this point, I can't tell if it is my dirty thoughts or the alcohol that has me blushing.

Lost in my own little day dream, I see fingers snap in front of my face. I shake my head back and forth; I`m pretty sure I have just been caught. *Shit! There goes my playing it cool routine.* "Em, what's up? I have been calling your name!" Annabelle yells at me. "Sorry," I croak out. Yep! It`s official! I was just caught staring at Jackson. That's embarrassing, maybe he didn't notice though. "I`m just tired, long drive and all," I say as an excuse. Looking up and around at everyone, I can`t help but notice that Mr. Jackass himself is smirking. *Crap! He caught me staring at him too!* God, that's really embarrassing. All I know is I have got to get out of here soon. Looking down at my watch, I see it is almost ten p.m.

Turning in my seat, I look over to Annabelle, "Can you show me which room is mine? I really need to get some sleep." *And take a cold shower!* Standing up to make my getaway, I take another quick peek around the table at everyone. *GASP!* He is still staring at me! *Actually staring!* Granted I did just stand up, but geez! I don't know if this is good or bad. Just the thought of him looking at me, makes me shiver. *Shit! Do you think he saw that?*

"Are you sure?" Annabelle pushes.

"Yeah." Oh that came out a little too fast to be convincing.

"Okay, I will show you to your room. Conner will you go grab her bags for her?" Annabelle asks.

"Sure babe," Conner says, immediately rising from his seat. "Keys?"

Throwing him my keys, he disappears from the room.

"Good night, I will see you guys in the morning," I tell everyone.

"Night," they all reply at different times, while Annabelle gets up from the table.

I follow her out of the kitchen and up the stairs.

"Are you sure you're all alright Emily? I honestly don't think he even remembers you. Although, I did see you staring at him," Annabelle says chuckling.

Muttering under my breath, I reply, "Yeah, I'm fine. Just tired. Maybe he doesn't remember me. And by the way, I was NOT staring!"

"Whatever," she says sarcastically.

The thought that he might not remember me, actually is worse. It's one thing to be embarrassed about something that has happened in the past. It's completely another if he doesn't remember me at all.

We make our way up the stairs and to the right where Annabelle starts quickly giving out everyone's sleeping arrangements. "Seeing how Conner and I are waiting until after the wedding to hook up again, we will be staying in different rooms. We gave the married couple, Brooke and Nathan, the master suite here," she says pointing to the first door on the left. "Jackson and Conner are staying in the room over there," she says pointing to the room down the hall on the right. "Since both guest rooms carry twin beds, I figured we would take the one in the middle here," she says opening up the door to our room. "The bathroom is the next door over. Unfortunately, we have to share with the boys, but it is only for four days."

Walking into the room, I find it is nice and quaint with plain white walls with twin beds on either side of the room. There is a window over the night stand, which sits in between the two twin beds. A white quilt sits at the bottom of each bed; it's the kind that makes you think of your grandmother's quilts in her house. But what catches my eye is the color of the bed sheets. They are the same color as Jackson's eyes. I find myself surrounded by things that make me think of him even when he isn't present. *SHIT!* Bet that's going to make me have dreams about him.

"That's fine. I don't mind sharing the bathroom," I assure her.

Hearing the front door slam shut, I see Conner lugging all three of my bags up the stairs.

"Geez Em! You are just as bad as Annabelle. We are only here for four days. Why do you need so much stuff?"

Chuckling, I reply, "It's a girl thing. We have to be prepared for anything." Setting the luggage in my room, he walks off calling, "Night." Annabelle gives me another hug before following behind him.

Walking over, I sit down on the edge of my bed. Taking off my shoes, I rummage through my suitcase for my pajamas. I guess it's not so bad. He didn't get up and walk away. Part of me is hurt that he didn't seem to recognize me though. But I could've sworn when he looked at me, it was as if he was trying to place me. I don't know, maybe this weekend won't be so bad after all. To him, I might just be a friend of the bride. But was I really that easy to forget? Did I mean so little to him? I guess it could always be worse. With that thought, I head off to locate the restroom with my bathroom bag. Might as well get into bed and get a good night's sleep. I have a whole new day ahead of me tomorrow.

# Chapter 3

## *That did not just happen*

I wake up the next morning to the sound of Annabelle yelling downstairs. For a girl getting married in a few days, she sure is angry. Next thing I hear is the sound of footsteps getting closer. Then my bedroom door snaps open, revealing Annabelle standing in the doorframe.

"Emily! Oh my gosh! What am I going to do?" She snaps.

Rolling over to my back, I let out an irritated sigh. It has got to be too early for this. The least a dreaded wedding week can give me is time to sleep in, right?

"EMILY!" She shouts, nudging my body back and forth.

"Hum?"

"The bakery called this morning and told me that, due to a stomach virus, their employees are sick and they won't be able to make my bridal shower cake for tomorrow. Can you believe that? And at this time my wedding cake is cancelled too! What am I going to do?" Annabelle explains.

"Cake isn't important at a bridal shower, sweetie. We can just pick up something cute at the store. As far as the wedding, maybe they will come through? If not, are there any other local shops you can call?" Is it me, or is it too early to discuss cake? I think coffee cake might be the only one that is appropriate at this time of the morning, and only cause it goes with coffee. *Yum! Coffee.* I could sure use a cup of that stuff right now.

"You have to have cake at a wedding. I have called around and nobody will do it on such short notice!" She demands. God she is feisty in the morning. Where does she get the energy?

"Fine, I will help and make a cake for the wedding."

Might as well get up! Moaning, I climb out of bed and rub my eyes. "But can a girl get a cup of coffee before we discuss specifics?"

"You will? Fantastic! Thanks." With that, she jumps up and runs out of the room screaming, "Conner, she's going to help us! I knew she would! Isn't this great?"

Pushing the hair out of my face, I grab my bathroom bag and head toward the bathroom. I do my quick normal routine in the morning that consists of brushing my hair and teeth and using the restroom. Feeling the desperate need for a cup of coffee, I don't pay attention to what I am doing. Throwing my bathroom bag over my shoulder, I open the door to the bathroom and run smack into what feels like a tree. But it's not a tree. It's hard, lean and warm to the touch. *Oh this can`t be good!* Slowly I look up and my mouth falls open when I realize I have run straight into Jackson. *SHIT!*

"Hi," he says.

My dear lord, I have both my palms flat on his chest. *Crap!* Snapping my mouth shut, I realize I still haven't responded. I can't seem to pull my thoughts together long enough to make a coherent thought. Who can blame me, I can actually feel his hard chest under his shirt. And it feels NICE! Biting my bottom lip, I notice he is still waiting for me to respond. "Um……" is what fumbles out of my mouth.

What the crap is um? Was I born yesterday?

I watch his lips slightly go up on the sides. Is he actually smiling? Great, now I'm starring at his lips. He does have such scrumptious lips. I wonder what it would feel like to kiss them and to taste them. Licking my lips, I realize I'm still staring at his mouth. *Crap!* Quickly looking back up into his eyes, I notice his eyebrows draw together and his smile getting bigger. He is flat out smiling at me! *Geez!* It's probably because I still haven't let go of his chest. What the hell is wrong with me? Oh yeah, it's because I'm the closest I have ever been to the love of my life, and I'm actually touching his well-defined chest. Closing my eyes, I take a deep breath. God, he even smells good. *Oh no!* Am I sniffing him now? Do you think he noticed? Please tell me he didn't!

Snapping my eyes back open, he asks, "You okay?"

*Of course not! I'm in your arms, practically fondling you!* Pull it together! "Mum hum."

Mum Hum! What is mum hum? Where's the simple; yes, I'm fine, great, or even yep? A nod would even work. Now I know I'm officially an idiot and so does he.

Jerking myself back, I remove my hands from his chest. The sudden movement causes me to stagger. His right hand shoots out and grabs ahold to my shoulder, steadying me. Dear lord, he is touching ME! The warmth of his hand sends a shiver rolling over my body. *I hope he didn't feel that.* Oh no! He probably did!

Looking down, I notice I am still in my pajamas. It's just a thin pink cotton camisole and shorts. Why didn't I think to put on something sexy, say a Victoria's secret baby doll? A bra at this point wouldn't be amiss. I should really invest in a robe, or at least remember to get dressed before I leave my bedroom.

Squeezing my eyes shut, I try to regain my composure.

Opening up my eyes, I glance up to find him looking at me curiously. *Man he is sexy!* With that thought, I really need to get away from him! I side step him and practically run like a dog after a bone back to my bedroom and slam the door shut. Standing with my back up against the door, I let out a breath of air. *Smooth, real smooth Emily. No wonder the guy turned you down all those years ago.*

Throwing my bathroom stuff on the bed, I rummage through my suitcases to find an outfit for the day. I decide on a pair of old faded blue jeans that are ripped at the knees. They are snug, but my butt looks high and tight in them. Donning a basic v neck grey t-shirt and my hot pink Aeropostal pullover sweater, I complete my look with my hot pink converse. I may have acted like a mute this morning, but I will go downstairs looking fabulous. Pulling my hair into a ponytail, I peek out my bedroom door. Okay, I may look fabulous, but it doesn't hurt to prevent another run in with him. When I see the bathroom door is shut, I open my bedroom door and haul ass downstairs to the kitchen. I`m just going to pretend that run-in didn't happen. I`m such an idiot! I see the `playing it cool` motto went right out the window. UGH!

Walking into the kitchen, I spot Annabelle, Brooke and Conner all standing at the island. They are drinking coffee and picking at what seems to be blueberry muffins. Looking around, I spot the Keurig on the counter. Making my way over to the machine, I grab myself a cup of coffee. I love these machines. I am going to have to buy one for myself one day. I keep saying that I will, but I never do.

Annabelle interrupts my thoughts, "Brooke and I decided that the girls are going to go into town to shop today. We can pick up everything you need to make the wedding cake while we are out. What are we going to do about the bridal shower though? We have to have some kind of dessert."

Pouring creamer into my coffee, I hear Brooke weigh in. "I was thinking cupcakes. They are the new thing these days. Totally hip."

Sneaking a peak over my shoulder, I see Annabelle has her nose crunched up. Smiling, I add a sugar to my coffee and stir.

"What do you think Emily?" Brooke inquires.

"Hum?" I say turning around, taking my first sip of coffee. It`s then I notice Jackson standing at the entrance to the kitchen. *Oh boy!* Looking away immediately, I try to act like I didn't see him. *Oh, please don't bring it up Jackson.* I wonder if he can see the pleading in my head for him to avoid what happened upstairs.

"I see you`re still at a loss for words this morning," Jackson says amusingly.

*I guess I'll take that as a no!* Choking on my coffee, I put down my cup and cover up my mouth. *Way to be cool! Geez!* He undoes me.

I watch Jackson saunter over towards me and the coffee pot. Peaking up at Annabelle and Brooke, I find them staring at me with curious eyes.

Annabelle chooses that time to pipe in, "You okay?"

"Yep, coffee just went down the wrong way," I reply quickly. Can I do anything around him that is normal? Taking a deep breath, I regret it immediately. *Oh, wow!* He showered and he smells absolutely divine. I wonder what type of cologne that is? Attempting to regain my composure, I pick up my coffee and take another sip. I have got to get away from him.

Of course Brooke won't let it go, "What do you mean `still`, Jackson?"

"Nothing," I answer for him. Jesus, I really need to learn to take a deep breath before I open my mouth.

Jackson laughs under his breath. *Great! Now he is laughing at me. Ugh.* Turning around with his coffee cup in his hand, he leans his hips up against the counter. Now he is standing right next to me. *Geez!* Trying to put distance between us, I take a step forward propping myself up against the island. "What do you think of the cupcake idea Annabelle?" I ask desperately needing to change the subject. At least now I can't smell him so much; however the mental picture of my hands on his chest will forever be etched into my brain for safe keeping. *Crap!* Now the cotton logo is running thru my head. (The touch, the feel, the fabric of our lives.) *Yeah! He could be my fabric!*

Thankfully Annabelle notices my change in subject but not before giving me the, *you will explain this later* look. That's going to be a great conversation. "I would prefer a cake," she says longingly.

Taking another sip of my coffee, I reply, "Okay, well we will see what cottons…" *Shit!* "I mean…cakes they have available." I am such an idiot! "What are you thinking about for the wedding cake?" Please tell me no one heard that.

Jackson finds this time to step up to the island next to me, grabbing a muffin. I can't help but look at his arms and hands over the top of my coffee cup. Those long fingers, I bet they will be good to, *AHHH*! Focus on cakes! Just drink your coffee and act normal for the love of god. Stop thinking of him and his hands.

Annabelle interrupts my thoughts, "We can go for something simple. I know its last minute. Speaking of, are you guys about ready to go? We don't have much time."

"I am," Brooke announces.

"Me too, let me just go grab my purse," I reply.

"Cool, I`ll meet you guys on the porch," Annabelle says.

Turning around, I put my coffee cup in the sink, while the other girls make their way out of the kitchen.

"Try not to run into anything else while you're out today," Jackson says with a smirk on his face looking directly at me. *Oh my god!* Is he flirting with me or mocking me? Blushing, I snap, "Thanks," and walk as quickly as my feet will take me out of the kitchen.

# Chapter 4

## *I think we got it all*

We spend the car ride discussing what kind of wedding cake Annabelle prefers. We decide to go with a simple design-- a classic white, three-tier round cake. Since red and white roses are her wedding flower, we decide to stop by the flower shop and ask if they could spare a few more. This way we could snip the stems off and put the actual rose buds in the middle of the tiers. It`s quick, easy and creates a gorgeous cake. Plus, the simplicity of the design will be manageable with the time we have before the wedding.

After the flower shop, we stop by a craft store and pick up the baking pans, fondant and cake decorating supplies. Then we head over to the grocery store to get the batter mix and icing for the cake. Annabelle decided to go with a marble cake with whipped frosting. It's not fancy, but desperate times calls for desperate measures. After picking up the cake mix supplies, we stop by a local bakery. We were able to find an adorable red velvet cake that was covered in a white marshmallow cream fondant, and wrapped in a gold trim ribbon. It has three full bloomed pink and white roses on the top to the left side. The bakery even managed to personalize it in gold with "To the new Mrs. LeBlanc" to the right of the roses. I even had to admit, for a last minute cake, I couldn't have chosen one better myself.

I actually thought I was out of the woods. Neither of them had made any comments the whole car ride into town about what Jackson had said this morning at breakfast. I should've known better. It was on the way home, after spending the whole morning shopping around town for supplies, that they held me ransomed in the car.

Annabelle speaks up first, "Okay, so enough is enough. We have avoided the situation too long. Spill it Emily?"

Man, just when I thought the coast was clear. Maybe I will try for denial. "I don't know what you are talking about?"

"Yeah, you do," Annabelle says firmly.

"No, really I don't," I say innocently.

"Seriously, the look that Jackson was giving you this morning, says something is up," Annabelle insists.

Brooke pushes, "Not to mention when he said STILL at a loss for words."

"It really was nothing," I say trying to deflect.

"Well, I don't know about you Brooke, but I want to know what that nothing is. How about you?" Of course you do Annabelle, you little nosy witch.

"Yep, I sure do!" Brooke agrees.

"Really guys…UGH. Fine! When I came out of the bathroom, I wasn't looking where I was going, and I kind of ran into him. Okay!"

"Like into him, into him?" Annabelle questions.

"Yes," I admit.

"Oh please tell me, what does his chest feel like, because it looks solid?" Brooke inquires.

She is happily married, why is she asking? Maybe she wants the mental picture I have cataloged in my head.

"Yes, it does look solid," Annabelle agrees.

Closing my eyes, "Guys!" This is going nowhere good!

"Just spill geez, it's just us," Annabelle pushes.

"So did it feel as good as it looks thru his shirt?" Damn that Brooke is a horny little girl isn't she?

"Yes okay, yes it did," I confirm.

That's what the problem was, it rendered me speechless. Realizing they weren't getting it, I decide I might as well spill the beans. Otherwise, face the torture of them all day.

"When he said hi, I was too focused on the fact that I was fondling his chest that I forgot to speak back. He had to ask me if I was okay, which I was. I was more than okay, but all I responded with was an umm." He must think I`m an idiot, because I sure do feel like one.

"So what happened after that?" Of course they wouldn't let it just end there. UGH!

"Yes, please continue," Brooke gestures for me to keep going.

"Nothing. I jumped back and ran away." Like the coward I am. There, I said all of it. How humiliating.

They both start laughing, before Annabelle asks, "You ran?"

"Yes, I ran. I was mortified!" I sure as hell wasn't going to stick around to embarrass myself anymore. That was for sure.

"I think he likes you," Annabelle states.

"I do too," Brooke agrees.

Well, I think they have both lost their mind.

"Yeah, did you see the look he gave her this morning? It was like `oh yeah, I could eat that!`" Annabelle says dramatically.

"Yeah, I kept checking to see if he was licking his lips, not that I was staring or anything. I am happily married," Brooke assures.

"Okay, stop guys, he doesn't like me!" For the love of god!  "He was looking at me because I was behaving like a lunatic this morning," I stress.

Rendered speechless by him I deduct as lunatic behavior. He also laughed at my stupidity, not to mention mocking me does not mean he likes me. This is not kindergarten. What are they thinking?

"I think you're wrong," Brooke announces.

"I do to," Annabelle confirms.

"Whatever, it doesn't even matter okay, I'm not interested," I say firmly.

"Yeah, that's like the pot calling the kettle black." Annabelle states, shaking her head back and forth.

"Why do you say that?" Brooke asks curiously.

"Cause she has been in love with him since she was fifteen."

Way to tell my life story Annabelle. Can a girl have any secrets? At all?

"Was in love, fell out of it at seventeen," I correct her.

"You just don't fall out of love," Annabelle snaps.

"You have a guy turn you down and you see how much resentment fills that void." Let me tell you it's a lot!

"Well, times have changed Emily, you have both grown up, you should go for it," Annabelle suggests.

"I think she should too. I know I would if I wasn't married, that boy is downright edible."

Is Brooke really licking her lips thinking about him? I mean, I am, but still.

"Tell me about it," Annabelle agrees.

"Can we stop talking about him? It's not going to happen okay. I refuse to be turned down again. Shame on you the first time, shame on me the second. I have learned my lesson. I'm going to stay far away from him." Why is this so hard for them to get? There is no way I could manage a second rejection from him.

"That's not a good plan," Annabelle remarks.

"I don't think so either. I think we need to put some aphrodisiacs out for them to eat. Maybe spark a mood," Brooke insists.

"Seriously guys, I`m not interested. Can we drop it?" PLEASE! I beg of you.

"Whatever you say Emily," Annabelle says annoyingly.

"Okay...," Brooke mutters.

"Thanks." I am so glad that conversation is over! Too bad we are now pulling up to the house.

# Chapter 5

## *Let's Bake*

Once we come to a complete stop, I find myself frantically looking around to count how many cars there are outside. *Why am I doing this?* This exact motto failed me last time. Oh well, time to suck it up. I told them I'm not interested, now I need to act the part. It is true though. When he turned me down all those years ago, I was completely devastated. My pride and self-esteem can't handle that again, much less my heart. Thinking back, it couldn't have been just about my age, could it? I know I was a few years younger, but it never came up when we hung out. Maybe I just wasn't his type. For what I could tell, he liked strippers. I know he dated quite a few of them. Yes, stripper strippers. I never understood how he could be attracted to someone who dances and takes their clothes off for money, but he was. He used to say they were just making an honest living. Whether you admit it or not, strippers in my book, will have sex for money. To me, they are just like a prostitute. Maybe that's why he liked them. I was no virgin at seventeen, but God I knew I wasn't experienced like him. He leaked of sex. I would've been open to him teaching me a few things though. Maybe that was the issue. He thought I was young and would require too much work, that I wasn't experienced enough. I know he knew I wasn't a virgin when I asked him to be more than friends.

I remember having a conversation with him one day in my house. He asked me about what turns me on and what I liked. I remember saying a guy's touch. A man with his hands on you doing the right thing can spark a fire deep inside. That, with a simple whisper in my ear, and I would have to go change my panties. He said his ears were his sensitive spot. You see, this is why I thought I had a chance with him. You don't have conversations like these with your so called male friends. God, I need to stop thinking about him before I lose it.

We get out of the car and start to unload the bags into the house. It's amazing how much damage three girls can make in a matter of hours.

"Oh wow, look at the time. I need to get to the bridal shop for a last minute fitting before I'm late. Want to go with me?" Annabelle invites.

"I'd love to!" Brooke squeals in excitement.

You would think it is her wedding day. Maybe she is just reliving it all over again.

"Sorry, I can't. I need to get started baking these cakes," I say.

"Okay, let me just go say bye to Conner and I'll meet you back at the car," Annabelle suggests.

"I'll go with you and say bye to Nathan. Where are they anyway?"

"They are cleaning up the barn. I want to have the family meet and greet hoe down out there, so they said they would

clean it up and then set up tables,"
Annabelle informs.

"That sounds fabulous. I have never heard of a family hoe down," Brooke says excitedly.

"Me neither," I utter. I'm not even sure what a family hoe down entails, but it does sound interesting.

They make their way to the barn, while I finish up unloading the groceries in the kitchen. Putting the bridal shower cake in the fridge, I walk back over to the groceries on the island. I sense movement out of the corner of my eye and look that way. Over the sink is a window that looks directly toward the barn. I see Annabelle and Brooke walking toward the men. I can't help but focus on Jackson standing there shirtless. SHIRTLESS! He sweeps his hand across his forehead, and then starts wiping them on his thighs. After saying bye to the girls, he resumes what he was doing. Bending down, his strong hands grab a hold to the table edge and lift. *HOLY SHIT*! Look at his big muscular arms flexing! I just keep following my eyes over his arms and down his chest to his mouth watering abdomen, where I find myself staring at his six pack. I didn't know those actually existed. He is sculpted to absolute perfection. I continue down and notice he is wearing a pair of blue jeans that ride low on his hips, showing you that he has the V. *Good god!* I just want to drag my fingers and tongue along each indentation his muscles make. I close my mouth, just for it to fall open again. I think I may actually be drooling. *Shit!* Wait, is that a tattoo I saw on his arm? I really need a closer look. *Oh No! No, I don't!* I need to focus and get back to the cakes. Shaking my head, I try to rid the thoughts in them.

I decide to grab my phone and flip through to my music. I need a distraction and music is just the thing. Placing the phone back on the counter, I turn up the volume as loud as it will go. Nothing like a little Justin Timberlake, "Rock Your Body", to clear your thoughts. Grabbing a big bowl and the cake mixes, I get to baking.

Lost in my own little world, Shakira "Hips Don't Lie" come on. We all know there is no way you can listen and not sing and dance along to that song. So that's what I am doing when I turn around and see Jackson watching me. His hips are leaning up against the door frame of the kitchen and his arms are crossed over his shirtless chest. *Crap!* Completely horrified, I stop dancing immediately and stand stark still. My eye balls have to be the size of golf balls right now. I can only imagine what color I have blushed to! I am like a deer caught in the headlights. Whatever you do, don't look down at his chest! Keep your eyes focused on his eyes! Don't try to locate the tattoo on his arm!

Maybe he didn't see me dancing. There's always a chance, right? Please god, let me have that chance.

"Don't stop on my account," he says amused.

Guess that answers that question. *Crap!* I can't move and I don't know what to say. What can I say? Sorry, I was just twirling my hips, shaking my ass,

singing into the batter spoon like a
microphone. *Oh sweet Jesus!* I`m still
holding the batter spoon. Closing my
eyes, I bite my lip. Maybe I can just
wish this moment away. Not the picture
of him shirtless standing in the kitchen,
oh no, I`m going to carve that picture
into my brain and keep it forever. I`m
talking about just the moment of me
being caught dancing.
"The cakes smell delicious," he says
reassuringly.
Great a change in the conversation. He is
throwing me a bone and I grasp at the
change in topic. Opening up my eyes, I
move over to my phone and turn off the
music. I don't need a reminder, that's for
sure. Keeping my eyes glued to the
island, I say hesitantly, "Thanks."
God, this is so awkward; I could just die
right now. Turning back toward the
cakes, I start stirring the batter
repeatedly. Might as well, seeing how I
am holding the batter spoon, aka,
microphone. Ugh. Why do these things
happen to me?

"Do you bake cakes as a profession?"
He asks.
Oh God, why is he making
conversation? Why can't he just turn
around and leave me to my humiliation?
"I wish, but no," I reply sincerely.
"So, a hobby then?" He inquires.
Still refusing to turn around, I stammer
out, "I...I guess." Great, now I'm
stuttering.

Walking over to the fridge, he opens it
up grabbing a water bottle before he
closes the door. Looking over toward
me, he says, "I can't wait to taste them."
Then he proceeds to walk out of the
kitchen.
*What the Hell?* Taking a deep breath, I
sigh out loud once I hear the front door
shut. *Way to go Emily.* Deciding not to
think about what he said or what just
happened, I get back to baking the last
cake. Ignorance is bliss right? This time
I don't turn on the music. I come to the
conclusion that the best thing I can do is
just finish in silence.

# Chapter 6

## *Is that what you're wearing*

I'm washing the last of the dishes when Annabelle and Brooke come breezing into the kitchen. They have with them what looks like enough food to feed an army. *Thank God!* Just the sight of food makes my stomach growl. I realize then that it is almost four p.m. and I haven't eaten yet.

"I decided to bring home food for us to eat. I got an assortment of sandwiches. I figured the bread would be good for us tonight since we will be drinking," Annabelle says.

She is the mothering type, always looking out for your best interest. You have to love that trait about her.

"Great I'm starving," I say smiling, as my stomach makes another loud sound. Digging into the food, I pull out a huge Turkey sandwich and go to town on it.

"What time are we heading out tonight?" I ask.

Tonight is Annabelle's bachelorette party. I have to say, I am thrilled to be getting out of the house and away from Jackson. The company of lots of girls and unlimited alcohol doesn't seem too bad either.

"The limo will be here at seven p.m.," Annabelle confirms.

"Why so early?" Brooke questions.

"They are coming here first, and then we are picking up several other people before we start the madness."

"Wait, we can drink in the limo right?" Brooke asks.

God, you have to love her. She never stops to think before she speaks. But then again, she is always asking the question you were thinking.

Chuckling, Annabelle replies, "Of course we are!"

Brooke grabs a sandwich and then makes her way to the front door while announcing, "I'm going to go let the guys know that the food is here!"

That's my cue! Shoving as much food in my mouth as I can, I wrap up the rest in a napkin. Glancing up, I see Annabelle is looking at me like I have lost my mind.

"Shower," I attempt to explain around the mountain of food in my mouth.

"Sure you're not just trying to avoid someone?" She asks jokingly.

Of course I am, but I'm not telling you that. Shaking my head no, I hustle out of the kitchen.

Moving swiftly into my room, I continue eating my sandwich while I pull together all my shower stuff. Once I have finished my sandwich, I grab my supplies and head off to the bathroom. No one is in there, which is awesome. Walking in, I put everything down and turn to lock the door, because I don't need anyone walking in, that's for sure. I take my time in the shower, shaving my legs to perfection. I don't plan on anyone touching them, but I'd rather be safe than sorry. Plus, the last thing I need is for Jackson to see my hairy legs. I think I have already embarrassed myself enough this weekend to last a lifetime already. Getting out of the shower, I feel like a million bucks. It never surprises me how good a simple shower can make you feel. Wrapping the towel around me, I grab my supplies and head toward my bedroom.

I spend the next two plus hours getting ready. Drying my long thick hair, I curl it in very small sections, giving me a dozen spiral curls hanging loosely down my back. My makeup is done up, giving me the look of smokey eyes. Since it`s a bachelorette party, I dress a bit on the sexy side. Deciding to wear a red strapless sweetheart top with a rouched bodice, I add my black mini skirt, which fits my body to perfection. Being that I am well endowed, the low cut sweetheart top I have chosen gives me great cleavage. Pairing it with a small red purse, I add my matching red high heels, putting on a few silver bangles and a pair of silver earrings. I spritz with my vanilla scented perfume. Adding some glitter vanilla scented lotion to my body, I look at myself in the mirror. I have to admit, I look sexy as hell.

Walking out of the bedroom, I realize I have a few minutes before its time to leave. I head to the kitchen to assess the cakes that I baked earlier. Finding that they have cooled off completely, I wrap them tightly in aluminum foil. Walking to the freezer, I begin making room for the cakes. I get two of them into the freezer when I turn around and see the last cake being handed to me. Glancing up, I find Jackson standing there looking down at me, holding the cake. I grasp ahold of the cake, but he doesn't let go.

"Is that what you are wearing tonight?" He asks.

Confused, all I can manage to do is nod my head up and down.

I don't get it? I am wearing the outfit aren't I? Isn't it pretty self-explanatory that this is what I am wearing tonight? Why does he care anyway?

His eyes flash. *Um, that can't be good!*

"Do you think that's a good idea?" He asks sternly.

"I don't know why it wouldn't be," I say honestly.

At my response, he takes a step closer to me, making my heart beat faster. The only thing separating us is a little four inch round cake.

Standing there, he looks down at me like if he is deciding what to say. I can't help but to stare into his beautiful blue eyes. Licking my lips, I notice his eyes drop to my mouth. *Holy shit! Is he going to kiss me?* Do I want him to kiss me? Who am I kidding? I have dreamt of him kissing me my entire life. Well, I sure as hell am not making the first move. Look where that got me last time.

Then I hear Annabelle shout down the hall, "Limos here!"

At the sound of Annabelle's voice, he backs up quickly. Dropping his hold to the cake, he disappears out of the kitchen. I stand there frozen in place for a few seconds before placing the last cake in the freezer.

Grabbing my purse, I head off toward the limo. I try not to think about what just happened, but how can I not? Was he going to kiss me? And what is wrong with what I am wearing? I thought I

looked sexy. Why does he even care
about what I wear?

Chapter 7

*I remember*

I wake up the next morning in my
bed with very little memory of last night.
*That can't be good.* Picking up the
covers, I look down at myself, finding
that I am wearing my pajama shirt and
panties. *That's always a good sign.*
Sitting up, I look around the room and
realize Annabelle isn't in her bed.
Maybe she slept with Conner in his
room. For having drunk as much as I did
last night, I feel surprising well,
especially considering I can't seem to
remember hardly anything. I decide in
that moment to go for a run. It's the best
way for me to clear my thoughts, or
remember them in this instance.

Getting up out of bed, I get dressed
in my running gear before heading off to
the bathroom to do my morning routine.
Once I am done, I stroll downstairs and
into the kitchen. No one seems to be
awake yet. Glancing at the clock in the

living room, I see it is ten a.m. *Wow*! I am up early. Oh well. Grabbing a water bottle from the fridge, I walk out the front door toward the driveway. I remember seeing a small path off the main road when I was driving in the other day, so I head in that direction.

I get up to a decent running pace by the time I hit the actual pathway. The path itself looks like it hasn't been used or tended to in a while. It`s an old concrete walkway that is lined with trees, along with over grown weeds and grass. The branches of the trees hover over each other, blocking a direct hit of the sunlight. It's peaceful right now. I bet at night it would be scary as hell though. I chuckle to myself at the direction my thoughts take me. Focusing on the smell of the leaves and flowers that are strong in the air, I slow myself down when the path starts to get steep. I stop by an old wooden fence and prop myself up onto it, deciding now is a good time to rest and take a few sips of my water.

Looking out into the woods, I can't help but try to remember what happened last night. I can recall the encounter at the freezer then heading off to the black stretch limo, where I got in and went straight for the tequila. That was my first mistake. Tequila and I don't seem to get along. It gets me drunk way faster than I think it should. I remember doing several shots and giggling a lot while we picked up the rest of our group. I know by the time we hit the first bar I was already stumbling. I blamed it on the high heels at the time, knowing it was mostly the alcohol. The drinks kept flowing while we were dancing, which I believe only improved our dancing skills and we were having a blast. *GASP!* I remember now! I remember what happened.

Annabelle drunk dialed Conner. Being a few sheets to the wind himself, he decided to cut his bachelor party off early and come to meet us, except he didn't come alone. No, he brought his whole party with him, which included Jackson. I didn't see Jackson at first because I was on the dance floor with another guy. We were dancing to Christina Aguilera's "Dirty". I remember Brooke nudging me and saying, "Damn, Jax is staring at you." Turning around, I looked in the direction where she was pointing, and sure enough, he was. Locking eyes with Jackson across the dance floor, I continued to dance with the other guy. It was like I was dancing with Jackson in my eyes. It was hot! I couldn't tell if Jackson was pissed or not, but I didn't put too much thought into it at the time. I just decided to give it all I had and essentially show him what he turned down all those years ago. Putting my hands in the air, I leaned my backside into the guy behind me. Grasping my hips with his hands, we swayed together to the music. I say swayed because it sounds so much better than grinding, but essentially that is what we were doing. When his hands started to move, one up and one down, I noticed a flash in Jax's eyes. Deciding to ignore Jackson's look, I turned around to face the guy I was dancing with, running my hands up his chest. His hands slowly drifted down my back, cupping my ass, pulling my body closer to him.

That was when a hand came out of nowhere, grabbing ahold to my arm. I was spun around quickly, causing me to lose my balance. Another hand shot out and grabbed ahold to my waist, steadying me. Startled, I looked up to see that I was now facing a very pissed off Jackson. *Opps!*

Looking over my shoulder at the guy I was just dancing with, Jackson growled, "Fuck off!" I cringed at the harshness of his voice. He then looked down at me and asked sternly, "What the hell were you doing?"

Being two sheets to the wind, I had the courage of an entire football field, so it didn't surprise me when I responded sarcastically without a hint of shame. Placing my hands on my hips I replied, "Dancing."

He didn't seem to like my answer. This was confirmed when he growled in my ear, "It looked more like you were trying to fuck him on the dance floor."

Why, are you jealous? Of course, I couldn't say that out loud, so instead I snapped back, "What's it to you?"

At my response he tightened his grip on my arm. Looking over my shoulder, he yelled to Conner, "Time to go!"

*Shit!* Trying to pry my arm free from him, I shot back angrily, "Let me go!"

Narrowing his eyes at me, he says rather irately, "No." Before I can respond, he leans further down to me, his voice laced with anger, "No woman should ever dance like that with another man. It gives him the wrong idea."

Having liquid courage, and not thinking before I speak, I lean up on my tip toes so that I'm face to face with him and respond sweetly with a hint of sarcasm, "I thought that's what you liked."

His eyes flash at my comment. I swear I could see the steam flowing from his ears. Letting go of my waist, he uses his grip on my arm to turn me. Placing his hand in the center of my lower back, he pushes me toward the front door.

I couldn't do anything at that point except follow his lead. His strong hand on my back was warm to the touch, instantly shooting tingles to all the right places on my body. *OH BOY!* I tried to concentrate more on walking than his touch. The last thing I wanted to do was fall flat on my ass in front of him.

When we reached the street, he ushered me directly to the waiting limo. Opening up the limo door, he shoved me inside. Sitting down in my seat, I was too pissed and drunk to do anything else besides sulk like a toddler while everyone else crammed in. One limo filled up with everybody going back to the house where we were staying, and the other limo filled up with everyone that had to be dropped off individually. When Jackson got in, he sat on the other side of the limo. He didn't look or say anything to me, which was perfectly fine by me. Why did he care if I danced with someone else? He had no right to stop me! He definitely didn't have a right to drag me out of the bar. Who did he think he was anyway?

Eventually my anger wore off and I passed out on the way home.

I remember being jolted awake when someone was lifting me. Opening my eyes, I find Jackson`s face was right in front of mine. I pull back quickly and his arms tighten around me.

"Stop!" He demands.

"What are you doing?" I ask, unsure of what is going on.

"I am carrying you to your room."

"Why?" I ask confused.

"You were asleep, and you can't stay in the limo all night."

*Oh!* Not having a good reply or the energy to walk, I rest my head on his shoulder. Closing my eyes, he continued to carry me to my bedroom. Taking a deep breath, I inhale his intoxicating scent. He smells like a mixture of sweat and cologne, absolutely divine. I had to admit, I liked being up against his hard chest. His arms around me, holding me, made me feel safe and wanted.

Opening up my bedroom door, he walks over to my bed, and lays me down gently. Rolling over immediately, I look up at him. He appears to be looking around the room for something, but I don't pay much attention. I am too busy thinking how much I like him being in my bedroom with me. That was until I had my pajama shirt shoved in front of my face.

"Put this on. You can't sleep in what you are wearing," he says, dropping my pajama shirt before walking out of the room.

I was barely keeping my eyes open. How was I going to get changed? But he was right, a strapless shirt and mini skirt were not ideal sleeping attire. Changing into the shirt, I laid back down falling asleep instantly.

Shaking my head back and forth, I try to push last night's thoughts out of my head. Standing up, I close the cap to my water bottle and decide to start heading back to the house. Walking up the steep path, my thoughts go back to last night. I'm officially more confused than I ever have been. It seemed as if he cared last

pg. 69

night. I have so many unanswered questions that I want him to anwser.

Trying not to think about all my questions, I remember his hand at my lower back. He has only touched me like that once before, when I was sixteen. We went to the movies to see "Saving Private Ryan." I remember sitting next to him in the chair, when he leaned over and whispered, "If you get scared you can hold onto me." I remember thinking to myself, why would I do that? I was such an idiot then. I should've just gone ahead and latched onto his arm right then and there. Oh well, can't change the past. When the movie ended, we got up and proceeded to the walkway. He put his hand in the center of my lower back and used it to guide me to the exit. His touch then gave me goose bumps all over my body, just like it did last night.

Pulling myself from my thoughts, I look up to find myself back in front of the house. Walking inside, I go straight upstairs to the bathroom. Without thinking or paying attention to what I am doing, I open the door and come face to face with Jackson.

# Chapter 8

## *I should learn to knock*

I knew I was wrong. Standing in my cropped black yoga pants and black sweatshirt that said "I don't sweat, I sparkle," I just couldn`t move. Even though I had sweat dripping down my face and body and my hair was a mess from running, I was frozen.
I stood in the door way, my hand holding onto the bathroom door knob, and just stared at him with my mouth wide open. He was buck naked. Yes NAKED! I couldn't even bring myself to do the respectable thing and look away. I have always wanted to see him naked, picturing it in my dreams more times than I care to admit. But seeing it in person was better than anything I ever could have imagined.

He was half way out of the shower and reaching for the towel when I opened the door. He seemed shocked for all of two seconds before he carried on with what he was doing, not seeming fazed by my presence. He reached for the towel and wrapped it around his waist, causing my eyes to wander to the direction where his hands were folding the ends of the towel into each other. I should've looked down before he wrapped himself up. *Damn it!* His brown hair was wet and dripping onto his broad shoulders. It was messy like if he had just ran his hands through it. He must have shaven in the shower because now his face was smooth and stubble free. His lips were full and curved up at the sides. I guess he finds me admiring his beauty amusing. *Oh well!* The water glistened off his athletic body, and I couldn't help but watch the water trickle over his chest and down his well sculpted belly. I noticed the hint of his tattoo on his arm, but I couldn't make out what it was. All I could smell was the scent of his shampoo or soap. I don't know what it was, but I found it arousing. Licking my lips, I discovered that my mouth was completely dry.

When he stepped forward and out of the shower, it brought me back to reality. Shaking my head back and forth, I try to concentrate. Taking another step toward me, I stepped back closing the door instantly. When the door was completely closed, I turned and ran to my bedroom. I was mortified. I couldn't believe that had just happened.

Plopping myself down on my bed, I cover my eyes. I still can't get over the fact that I just walked in on him in the shower and he let me just stare at him. He acted like he thought it was amusing. That he didn't mind if I stared at him like a piece of meat. I mean, he has nothing to be ashamed of from what I saw, but still. Who does that? Who doesn't lock the door when they know they are sharing a bathroom with others? I should really learn to knock when I see the door closed from now on. Not that I wouldn't want to see that again, trust me I would. I just don't want him getting any ideas that I could or would go there.

The way he behaved last night was beyond crazy. I know that I practically asked for it staring at him while I danced with that other guy, but he had no right to say the things that he did. He doesn't own me and I can dance how I want or with who I want. Or as he called it, practically fucking a guy, anywhere I want. It is my choice. I gave him the opportunity to have a say when I was seventeen, and he turned me down. He made a choice then because he didn't want me, so why is he acting like he might now?

I can't be blindsided by the things he does or says again. I remember when I was sixteen, I had come home from hanging out with friends and found him waiting for me in my driveway. I was upset at one of my friends about something, I don't remember what. But when he asked who, I went and grabbed a picture. The picture had three friends of mine in it, plus me. When I showed him the picture he made a remark "Your friends are pretty, but only one of them is extremely beautiful in my eyes." I remember it made my day. He did that a lot, always making me feel special and pretty. That's why I thought he liked me then.

Another time when I was seventeen, I was in my bedroom and I couldn't find anything to wear to church that night. Everything I tried on made me feel fat or ugly. I was standing in front of my full length mirror when he came into my bedroom. He walked over to me and asked me what was wrong. I rolled my eyes and said, "I can't find anything to wear." He looked me up and down, before saying, "I think you look amazing in what you are wearing." I wore that outfit to church that night. A few words from him and I was mush. I can't let him do that to me again. I don't want to get lost in all that is him just to be shot down again. I'm still the same person I was back then. I decide it is in my best interests to just avoid him at all cost. And if I can't, then I need to act like he doesn't faze me through the rest of the wedding week. Then I can go home and resume my life. *I can do this!*

Knowing he was probably out of the bathroom by now, I decide to grab my stuff and go take a quick shower. When I`m done, I dress in a pair of blue jean shorts with a navy blue tank top. I love this tank top because the back is see-through and it has lace trimmed roses etched all over. I pair it with a brown belt and brown sandals. Knowing that I have to do my hair for tonight's family hoedown, I just throw it on top of my head and pin it in a messy knot. I know pieces are falling out everywhere, but I don't care. I don't have anyone to impress.

Making my way downstairs I head into the kitchen. I haven't eaten today and I can hear my stomach protest at this very moment. I go to the fridge and find the left over sandwiches. Grabbing one, I make my way over to the island to eat. I`m halfway through my sandwich when Jackson walks in. Looking down, I focus on what I have left to eat, trying to ignore him. He makes his way behind me, placing a cup into the sink. Keeping my head down, I think to myself this is working when I feel the heat of his body radiating behind me. Taking a deep breath, I try not to panic. He places his hands on each side of me on the island. I can feel my pulse pick up and my heart feels like it is going to fly out of my chest. Biting my lip, I close my eyes and sense him lean into me. His front is pressing up against my back and I am frozen in place. I try not to focus on the warmth of his body or the smell of his shampoo. Softly he whispers in my ear, "I'm glad I didn't lock the door."

The sound of his voice emits goose bumps all over my body, and the feel of his breath on my neck causes my nipples to harden instantly. I find myself frantically waiting to see what he will do next. At this point, I'm doing everything I can manage just to keep myself standing upright. Trailing his nose from the tip of my ear and down my neck, I shiver and my knees give out. Moving one hand from the island, he wraps it around my waist to steady me. I tilt my head to the side, allowing him better access. When I feel his lips curve up into a smile on my neck, I realize that he knows he has me.

He plants a quick kiss to my neck before releasing me and walking out of the kitchen. My mouth drops open and I let out the breath of air that I didn't know I was holding. I look aimlessly around the room. Did that just happen? Yes, yes it did. I can still hear my heartbeat in my ears as proof. I know one thing for sure, if he would've done one more thing, I think my panties would've self-combusted. Poof! Gone! Swallowing hard, I try to compose myself. It's not working and I need to go take a cold shower, or at least put on a new pair of panties. Why would he do that? Why did I let him do that? Is this a game to him?

I pick at the rest of my sandwich in front of me, but I'm no longer hungry for food. I don't know what just happened or why. Part of me wants to go find him and demand he finishes what he started. I know that is a bad decision though. So instead, I push the thoughts aside in my head and go search for Annabelle. I know there will be something I can help her do for the wedding or bridal shower. At this point, all I need is any type of distraction and one that doesn't come in the form of Jackson.

# Chapter 9

## *Let me help*


I find Annabelle in the barn. She is barking out orders as if she is the recruiter and her fiancée and friends are a bunch of new recruits. I snicker to myself when the thought of Bridezilla comes to mind. Yeah, she makes a good Bridezilla. I doubt I will be like that if I ever get married, `if` being the prominent word. She has a clip board in her left hand and is waving a pen in her right hand, like it is a wand with magical powers that will make everyone move. It is working though; I have to give her credit for that.

Walking over to her, I ask, "Anything I can help with?"

She looks at me peculiarly and says, "Of course! How's the cake coming along though?"

"It's good. The cakes are baked and freezing at the moment."

"Freezing?" She interrupts.

I smile; I can tell the thought makes her nervous.

"Yes, freezing. If you bake them, then place them in the freezer overnight, they come out moist the next day."

"Oh!" She says surprised.

It amazes me that more people don't know that is how grocery stores and bakeries function.

"Tomorrow I will pull them out and start to work on decorating them," I assure her.

"Will you be done in time?" She asks apprehensively.

"Yes, all I have to do is ice the cakes. Make sure they are leveled, and then spread a quick layer of fondant over them."

"It sounds like a lot of work still," she says doubtfully.

"It is, but it is manageable." It really is, it will be another couple hours of work, but none of it can be done today. Thankfully I don't have to make designs. Just throw some roses on top and wall la it's done. A simple classic masterpiece.

"So, what can I do to help?" I need to get off the subject of the cake. I don't want her to stress about it anymore than she already is.

"Well, the flower guy called and his van broke down. Do you think you can go grab the flowers the morning of the wedding? I understand if you can't with the cake," she says hesitantly.

"The majority of the cake will be done tomorrow sweetie, so I can swing in town and pick up the flowers the morning of the wedding. What can I do today though?"

It seems she doesn't want to ask me to do anything, because she is already giving me the burden of making the wedding cake. We fought about this when she first got engaged. She wanted me to make the cake, but I told her no, that I wasn't good enough. She begged to differ and told me I was never going to make my dream happen of owning my own bakery if I didn't put myself out there. I finally convinced her that I wouldn't be able to enjoy myself if I had to stress over the making of her wedding cake. Honestly, I was worried I would screw it up and it wouldn't be pretty enough… I still am.

She looked at her clipboard and seemed to be studying it for a while. Then looking up at me, she says, "Would you mind setting up the living room for tomorrow's bridal shower?"

"Sure," I reply quickly. I can do that, plus it gets me away from all things Jackson.

"I'll have one of the men bring you a couple tables to set up. Just decorate the living room how you see fit and that would be a huge help."

"You don't have an outline of where you want everything to be placed on that clipboard of yours?" I ask sweetly. She seems to have everything else on that thing, so I wouldn't be surprised.

Smiling she says, "Nah, I just sketched a picture of the barn for the hoe down and then the reception. I didn't even think to do the bridal shower."

"So, just what the men have to set up is what you sketched?" I ask peculiarly.

We started laughing at the fact that this is what she actually did.

It feels good to laugh. It seems this weekend has just been so tense with everything going on. Looking up and around, I see Jackson on the ladder. His hands are wrapped around a white lantern light and his eyes are fixed on me. It is as if he is studying me. I stare at him for a quick minute, before looking back to Annabelle. Unfortunately, she notices him as well.

"Why is he staring at you like that?" She asks confused.

"I don't know, I was thinking the same thing?" I say unsure myself.

"It is like he didn't recognize you?"

"That's what I was thinking too? Strange isn't it?" I agree.

"Has anything else happened between you two since the other day?" Annabelle inquires.

"What? No?" There I go snapping back responses.

She smiles as I feel the heat spread up to my cheeks.

"So no more run in`s with him then?"

"Nope." I swear I can't lie to save my soul.

"Has he said anything to you?" She knows I'm lying.

*God!* I hate being an open book.

"What do you mean?" I say, attempting to evade her question.

"You guys haven't talked?" She asks, tilting her head to the side and focusing on me.

"Why would we? I have nothing to say to him. Now where is the bridal shower stuff so I can get started on it?" I am already over this conversation and need to get away.

"Okay, I'll let this go for now," she concedes. "The shower stuff is in the corner of the living room. Also, some decorations are in the trunk of Conner's car. And my keys should be on the table next to the front door," she says with a small smile.

She knows that I am keeping something from her. But, being a good friend, she leaves it until I am ready to talk about it. At least she isn't pushing it for now.

"I will go get started," I inform her, walking off quickly without another word. *Great!* Now I'm going to have to talk to her. Maybe I can just keep turning the conversation back to the wedding to distract her? That, or start pointing out things the men are doing wrong and turn her into Bridezilla. I know it would be throwing others under the bus, but hey, it would buy me more time.

Making my way into the house, I grab Annabelle's keys from the front table and head toward Conner's white Ford Fusion. Opening up the trunk, I find that it is completely full. Where did she put her luggage? I wouldn't be able to get one thing in here even if I tried. Oh well, might as well get started. Grabbing several bags, I head back toward the house. Once inside, I decide to put the decorations next to the stairs. I might be blocking the way to the kitchen but, I don't want to place them in the living room where I will be working. Turning around to head back out the door, I see Jackson walking up the steps.

"Annabelle said you needed a few tables. Where do you want me to set this one up?" He inquires.

"Oh, um. I haven't exactly thought about where I want to put them yet. Can you just lean them up against the wall here?" I say, pointing to the wall on the other side of the stairs.

"Sure," he says deadpan.

Something is up with him. He isn't showing me any emotion. Not to mention the way he was looking at me in the barn. Did I piss him off? Wait, why would I care if he's pissed? I'm supposed to be ignoring him. So, why does it bother me so much?

Not knowing what to say, I mutter a quick, "Thanks," and walk out the front door to grab more bags.

We don't say anything to each other when he brings in the next table. Come to think about it, we don't even make eye contact. I know I wanted to avoid him, but this just feels wrong. I decide to keep my mouth sealed shut for now though.

It wasn't until he brought in the third and final table that he spoke to me. And when he did it was still laced with very little emotion. He didn't even look at me when he said, "Just let me know when you decide where you want them and I will come back." With that, he walked out the front door and back to the barn. I didn't know what to think of the whole thing. Something was bothering him, but it wasn't my place to ask. I decided to busy myself with the bridal shower preparation and not think about it.

I worked for what seemed like hours on decorating, but when I was done, it was absolutely beautiful. I had pushed the living room furniture up against the wall on one side and got rid of any knick knacks that weren't important, placing them in the garage. Once I had the room cleared out and furniture placed, I set up one table across from the furniture. Since only one would fit in the living room without making it look to overcrowded, I used the other two in the formal dining room. I pushed the dining room table slightly closer to one side and used the two tables up against one wall. I had it set up like a buffet. I figured we could place the food and bridal shower decor in the dining room, and use the one in the living room for games and presents. I covered all the tables with pink table cloths. It seemed her bridal shower theme was a pink and white, blushing bride concept.

I went thru what food there was and picked containers for them, and placed the containers on the table where I wanted them set up. Then I moved the food onto the formal dining room table, since it could stay there until we needed it. She had fake pink and white roses that I placed in vases and arranged in different areas around the living and formal dining room. I didn't blow up the balloons, but I did hang the confetti and pink puffy balls that she had. When I was done, I was astonished at what I had created. I had transformed the room into a pink and white party palace.

Annabelle came into the living room shortly after I had finished, followed by Conner, Brooke, Nathan and Jackson. I was still standing admiring the beauty that I had created before me when I heard Annabelle gasp.

"It looks amazing Emily. You have a knack at making things beautiful. Never in my wildest dreams did I imagine something so lovely." Annabelle states, clearly happy.

Turning around to face her I reply, "Thanks. It was fun, and I have to say, I am pretty impressed myself."

Annabelle comes closer to me and whispers in my ear, "Between you and me, I am happy I didn't make you a sketch to go by."

At this comment, we start giggling. Glancing up, I see everyone staring at us, like we have lost our minds. *Oh well.*

Conner interrupts, "Sorry to bust your bubbles ladies, but if you guys want to be ready in time for the family hoedown, I think you need to start getting ready now."

Looking down at my watch, I couldn't agree more. We have less than two hours to shower and get ready. It may seem like a lot of time for most people, but it takes precious time turning myself into a masterpiece, especially with the amount of hair that I have. At that, the girls and I move toward the stairs to get started while the men head to the kitchen since it only takes them ten minutes top`s to get ready. I don't think I will ever not be pissed off about that.

# Chapter 10

## *Jealous much*

I take a long shower doing all the things girls do right before a hot date: trim, pluck, shave. You know, all the things that leave a woman feeling confident and sexy. I`m not going on a date, but after this morning's event in the kitchen, I want to be safe and prepared for anything. Not that I was expecting something to happen, I wasn't, it was more of a `just in case.` Oh, who am I kidding? If he traps me like that again, there is no way I am going to say no.

I get dressed in a pair of low riding daisy duke cut off blue jean shorts, pairing it with a tiny, form fitting, flannel button up shirt that I tuck into my shorts. Annabelle has bought us adorable cowgirl boots; they are brown and have a flower design etched along the sides. To tie my outfit together, I add my big brown belt.  My hair is in big wavy curls that I let flow loosely down my back. I keep my makeup light and decide against jewelry. It might not sound fancy, but I have to tell you, I looked HOT! All I needed was a cowboy hat to top off my outfit and I was every cowboys dream come true.

Walking downstairs I hear the sound of country music coming from the barn. Heading that way, I recognize the song playing as Kenny Chesney "Shift Work" Hum… Kenny sure is sexy. Why are singers so sexy? Think about that Kenny, Justin Timberlake, Brad Paisley, and Tim McGraw? I should switch my profession as a nurse and get in the music business. With those thoughts in my head, I walk into the barn.

What used to be an old red barn smothered in hay bales and spider webs is now breathtaking. Round white decorative lantern lights hang from the top of the barn illuminating the place. I stand for a minute admiring all that is going on. Looking around, I see a DJ on the left hand side close to the entrance. In the middle of the room is a huge dance floor. I remember the guys having this conversation at the table the first night I arrived. They had bought several boxes of hardwood flooring at the local hardware shop and laid them out. They spent over two hours piecing them together and then made a boarder around it, so it wouldn't move. Their hard work has paid off.

To the right is a make shift bar that they have made as well. The men definitely have skills when it comes to their woodwork. In the back of the barn they have set up long tables with chairs on each side. The tables are topped with white table cloths and have several mason jars going down the middle of the table. Every other mason jar either has a tea light candle shining in it or has white daisy's flowing from them. I found the entire set up to be completely romantic.

Making my way over to the bar where they have hired a bartender, I order a Cape Cod with a splash of pineapple juice. Turning around, I face the dance floor. The crowd in the middle is line dancing and the people along the

outside are two-stepping. I notice
Annabelle and Conner are in the middle
of the floor, while Brooke and Nathan
are two-stepping on the outside.
Grabbing my drink, I take a sip thinking
about how they both make such
awesome couples.

Looking around, I spot Jackson in the
corner of the room with a black cowboy
hat on. He is wearing a black and white
flannel shirt that hugs his arms and a
pair of blue jeans. The top few buttons
are undone on his shirt, revealing a
glimpse of his magnificent chest. Just
seeing him makes me flash back to when
he was getting out of the shower and
then our encounter in the kitchen.
Licking my lips, I am about to head that
way when I see a girl approach him. She
is very courageous seeing how she walks
right up to him and places her hand on
his chest. He doesn't attempt to push her
away; instead he looks down at her and
smiles. He then reaches for her hand,
leading her out onto the dance floor.
She's very pretty, with her short brown
hair that stops just below her ears and

her amazing tan. I feel like I'm going to be sick to my stomach. I realize then that I'm jealous. I want to be the one in his arms dancing with him. I know he's not mine, yet I feel like we have a connection. I suddenly have the urge to go pry out her eye balls and smash cupcakes down her throat. Maybe if I make her fat and ugly he won't like her. Turning to the bartender, I get myself a shot of tequila. I knew I was going to need a little more than the vodka in my Cape Cod to help me get thru the night if I had to watch this.

I watched them two-step on the dance floor to Brad Paisley "Mud on the tires". It isn't a dance where you are all over each other, but I do find it can be a very intimate dance when you want it to be. And in that moment I knew I wanted it to be intimate between him and me.

I remember when I was sixteen, it was after church and we were hanging out in front of his truck. He asked me if I knew how to dance and I said Yeah, but I didn't know how to spin. He then got up and walked to his truck, putting in a

CD. Turning the music up, he walked back over to me and held out his hand, asking me to dance. I recognized the song immediately as Tim McGraw's "Where the Green Grass Grows". He sang the song to me while we danced. Of course, we kept laughing every time he went to go spin me and I would lose my balance, but other than that it was so romantic. At the end of the song, he said, "I love this song and I agree you can't spin. At all." Now every time I hear that song, I think of him on that night and smile to myself.

When the song was over, another girl went right up to Jackson and asked him to dance. It was as if they flocked to him. This was ridiculous—one, me being jealous, and two, the way they went after him. I knew he was hot, but geez. This time it was a cute blonde girl. Her hair was a couple of inches below her shoulders and it was bright blonde. You could tell she had a fake rack, but damn I'd be lying if I said they didn't look good on her. What's worse is I love this song; it's Darius Rucker's "Wagon

Wheel". With a little alcohol to guide me, I decided it was time to get even.

Off I went to go find myself a young strapping cowboy to dance with. I found one immediately; he was shy but I didn't care. I led him to the dance floor and we started two-stepping. He turned out to be a shitty dancer. I had to end up leading him by saying left, left, right. It didn't help that he seemed to have ten left feet. I didn't care though, I love dancing even if it is with a crappy sidekick.

I found a new partner for the next dance. His name was Joseph and he could dance. He could also lead me very well, which made me look like I could actually dance and twirl. My favorite was to "Footloose". He twirled me so much during that song I was dizzy, but I didn't care. I was having a blast. I wasn't paying attention to Jackson, I was just enjoying myself. I even danced a few songs with Annabelle, including Brad Paisley`s "Ticks", where I came up with my own hand movements to implicate the words.

When Faith Hill comes on, I decide to take myself to the bar to get another drink. Every time I hear Faith Hill, I think of Jackson. We used to have heated arguments about who we thought was hotter back in the day. I used to think it was Shania Twain; he would argue and say Faith Hill. I still don't know who won those battles, but I'd like to think it was me.

I was at the bar sipping my drink when Jackson approached me. He ordered himself a beer and I decided to chug the rest of mine, needing the liquid courage. When the bartender gave him his beer, he took a sip before looking over at me. With a smile on his face he said, "I see your dancing has greatly improved."

All I could do was look up at him and smile. When the song changed over to Lone star "Amazed", he extended out his hand asking me to dance. I took it without thinking twice. Leading me out to the middle of the dance floor, he let my hand go. I just stood there feeling a little uneasy for a brief second. Then he slid his arms around my waist, so I wrapped mine around his neck. Pulling me close, we started swaying to the music. When he started singing the song in my ear, I felt my whole body relax into him. By the end of the song my head was leaning on his shoulder. I didn't want the song to end. For a brief moment it was like I had been transported back in time to us dancing in the church parking lot, to the time before I told him how I felt about him and was rejected. Back before it all essentially went to crap.

When the song ended, Rascal Flatts "Life is a Highway" came on. Since I was enjoying myself, I was pretty depressed the song was over and I had to stop dancing with him. Removing my hands from his neck, I turned to leave. He grabbed my hand and spun me back around before I could even step away. "I thought we were dancing," was all he said, before he proceeded to drag me to the outside of the dance floor. Stopping abruptly, he turned toward me and immediately put his hand on my hip.

Pulling our conjoined hands up to his chest, we started two-stepping with everyone else. It wasn't slow dancing, but I would take what I could get. I was close enough to smell his cologne and I was touching him, so I really couldn't complain.

We danced like two people unsure of what to do or say to each other. We were just going through the motions of the dance. It wasn't intimate like the slow dance, but it wasn't the laughing and having a good time like it was in the past either. It was awkward to say the least. When the song ended, I knew I had to get away. I wiggled my fingers to try to get him to drop my grip, but he didn't. He glanced down at our conjoined hands that were resting up against his chest before he looked back up into my eyes. I tried to pull away but his arm around my waist tightened, pulling me closer to him. He studied me for a few seconds and I closed my eyes. I didn't know what he was thinking, but I knew I couldn't handle this. I wanted him but I didn't want to go down that road again, especially if it was going to be awkward. Opening my eyes, I tried to pull away once more, but he wasn't having it. Holding me in place, he tilted his head down, pressing his forehead against mine. He was so close that if I leaned up on my toes I could probably kiss him, but I wasn't going to go there. Not now at least.

Softly he whispered, "What are you scared of?"

I whispered back the only thing I could think of, which was the honest to god truth, "You."

His eyes flashed. I don't know if it was shock or anger, but he let me go immediately. I walked swiftly off the dance floor and headed toward the exit.

# Chapter 11

## *Leave it to Annabelle*

I hit the exit of the barn but instead of going left toward the house, I head to the right. I know there is a wooden fence that encloses fields of flowers in the distance, so that's where I go. Propping myself up on the fence, I let my mind wander. I am confused. This morning he seemed so mad at me, but I still don't know why? I could tell at the beginning of the hoe down he was avoiding me. It was only after a couple of songs on the dance floor that I saw him start to look my way every so often. I also can't believe how jealous I got of the other girls dancing with him. I had no right to feel that way. I'll admit my slow dancing with him is a dream come true. Not to mention being in his arms just feels so right to me. But, I still don't know what changed between the slow dance to the two-step. I know I was nervous and a little unsure of how to act.

At least when he asked me what I was scared of, I told him the truth. I am terrified of him, terrified that my heart is going to be broken all over again. It took too long to repair the first time, I don't think I can manage it again. But when I look into his eyes, I`m mystified. His eyes are like pools of blue silk that completely engulf me. I want to go there, but then I remember the pain of him leaving and I back off.

My thoughts are quickly halted when I hear the sound of a stick splintering. I jump, turning around quickly to see what made the noise. All I can think of are those scary movies where a blonde is all by herself. I'm going to die, just like all those girls in the Jason movies.

When I see it is just Jackson, I sigh in relief.
"I didn't mean to scare you," he says.
"You didn't," I lie immediately.
"Right," he replies sarcastically.
Hopping up onto the fence next to me, we sit in silence. It is a little awkward, but I like him next to me so I don't complain.

He mumbles under his breath after a few minutes, "I'm sorry."
The words tumble out of my mouth before I can take them back, "For what?"
"Everything," he says sincerely, exhaling loudly.

He truly does sound sorry. Gazing up at him, I ask, "Why were you mad at me earlier today?" I can't help it, I want to know. What did I do wrong? How did I upset him?
"Ah that," he replies hesitantly as he looks away from me, shaking his head. I start to think he isn't going to answer, but then he takes a deep breath and responds honestly.
"I wasn't mad at you. I was mad at myself. When I heard you laugh, it was nice. You have such a beautiful laugh." Twisting his head, he looks back at me and smiles. "When you laugh, I can't help but smile. Your whole face lights up." Turning back toward the field, he continues. "You used to laugh all the time. I couldn't help but think the reason you aren't laughing now is because of

me. It pissed me off to think I was doing that to you."

*WOW*. My laugh makes him smile. That`s sweet. I don't know how to respond to him though. I know he is waiting for me to either admit it is true or deny it, but I can't. Biting my lip I look back out into the field. This is so different, we used to be around each other all the time and it was never awkward, nor a dull moment. I should've kept my mouth closed all those years ago. His friendship would have been better than not having him at all, right?

We sit in silence for a while, until I hear Annabelle shouting my name from the barn doors.

"EMILY!"

Turning my head toward her, I holler back, "Yeah!"

"There you are. I was looking all over for you. Our song is on, now get your ass inside and dance with me."

Shaking my head back and forth, I can`t help the grin on my face when I look over at Jackson.

Smiling, he says, "We better not keep her waiting."
Climbing off the fence, we make our way to the barn doors where Annabelle is located. Leave it to Annabelle to break an awkward moment. The girl truly has a gift.

When we get closer, we find Annabelle dancing with herself and singing at the top of her lungs to Taylor Swift`s "We Are Never Ever Getting Back Together". Deciding to join her, I make my way to the dance floor. We are having a blast, dancing and singing at the top of our lungs, that it doesn't faze me when Jackson and Conner join us. Lost in the moment when the song changes, I don't hesitate when Jackson grabs my hand, pulling me into him and we start two stepping to Zach Brown Band`s "Chicken Fried". This time it is different than before when we danced. We are laughing and singing loudly while we make our way around the floor. It helps that Annabelle and Conner are right next to us, singing and dancing as well. It is like the mood was broken from earlier. We are all just having a good time and going with the flow.

We dance to several more songs after that. When the DJ announces last song, I'm immediately a little heartbroken. I realize that I haven't laughed this hard or had this much fun in a really long time. When the music changes to Brad Paisley`s "She's Everything", Jackson instantly pulls me closer. Wrapping his arms around my waist, we begin slow dancing to the music. I don't look at him; I just rest my head on his shoulder and breathe in his scent. I want to enjoy this moment as much as I can before it comes to an end.

I am unsure of what to do once the song ends. Do I stay put and see if he makes conversation, or do I ask him if he wants to go for a walk? Should I just leave and go back to my room? No, I definitely don't want to do the last one. I want to spend more time with him, but how do I make that happen? When the song finally comes to an end, I tilt my head back, and look up into his beautiful eyes. He looks at me for a brief second before his left hand drop`s from around my waist. Feeling the loss immediately, I bite my lip. I think he is going to pull away and I don't know what to do or say.

Reaching up, he grabs ahold to my hand at his neck and says softly, "Come with me."

At a loss for words, I nod my head in approval. Dropping his right hand around my waist, he walks off the dance floor still holding my hand. I don't know where we are headed and personally I don't care. *Jackson is holding my hand, ekkk!* Smiling to myself, I follow him.

Surprisingly we head toward the house. When we make it through the front door and up the stairs, I really start to get confused. Are we about to have sex? Cause, I don't know if I'm ready to go there. I mean, I wouldn't say no or push him off if he tried. Maybe he is just walking me to my door. *I would rather have sex.* God, even my subconscious is sounding like a whore now. When we get to my door, he turns around to face me. *Oh god!* Stepping closer to me, he brings our bodies together. He advances again leaving me no choice but to step back until I am up against the wall. Raising our joined hands up, he places them above my head. Taking a deep breath in, I bite my lip. He has me pinned up against the wall. *YAY!* Closing my eyes, I can feel the warmth of his body all over mine. Suddenly I feel his right hand on my neck. Opening my eyes, I find his warm, soft, lust filled eyes are fixated on me. He drops his eyes to watch his thumb slowly drift from the corner of my ear, along my jaw, stopping at my bottom lip. I swallow, struggling to control my own breathing. Listening to my heartbeat pounding in my ears, my eyes slowly drift down to his lips where I watch him lick his bottom lip. *Damn, I want to do that for him.* Bringing my left hand up, I grab ahold to his shirt at the waist, attempting to bring him closer to me. I know he gets the hint when he leans further into me, brushing his lips softly against mine. Pulling his head slightly back, he whispers, "I have wanted to kiss you for as long as I can remember." Before I know what is happening, he releases me and says, "I'll see you tomorrow baby, sweet dreams." With that, he turns and walks off to his room, shutting the door behind him.

# Chapter 12

## *He wouldn't would he*

I look up into his eyes and see the warmth in them. He wants me. My heart is racing and my legs feel weak. His lips move down to meet mine. They are gentle and soft, yet his kiss is passionate and aggressive. His tongue thrust into my mouth and my knees buckle. He catches me before I fall by wrapping his strong arms around me, pressing me into him. I wrap my arms around him, feeling every curve and muscle of his back. Making my way down to the top of his jeans, I start pulling at his shirt. Breaking the kiss, he helps me by yanking his shirt over his head. Moving his body back to me, he starts kissing my neck. A moan escapes my mouth. I can't help it, my body aches for him. Pressing my body closer to his, I feel his hand slide from my back and under my shirt. His hand heads toward my breast. KNOCK KNOCK KNOCK.

I'm jolted awake, panting with an undeniable ache between my legs. KNOCK KNOCK KNOCK. *Holy Shit!* Someone is at my door. Looking around, I realize it was just a dream. *Damn!* It felt so real. Swinging my legs over to the side of the bed, I stand up. Rubbing the sleep from my eyes, I walk to the door and open it up, finding Brooke on the other side.

"Hi. What are you doing here Brooke?" I say surprised.

"Well, seeing how it is only an hour and a half prior to the bridal shower, I thought I would wake you up. Are you sick?" She says studying me.

"No, why?"

"You're all flushed. Do you have a fever?"

*GASP!* "What? No... No, I'm not sick, no fever," I say quickly.

What am I supposed to say, Oh, I was just dreaming about being fondled by Jax? Oh dear lord, I'm going to hell. "I need to get ready," I say quickly turning around and grabbing my shower bag. "Thanks for waking me." Making my way past her, I head into the bathroom without another word.

I take a quick shower and dry my hair straight. The bridal shower is informal, so I choose to go with a pair of white skinny jeans and a white short sleeve button up shirt. I top it with a tan form fitting halter vest that sits just under the top of my breasts. Donning a pair of tan high heels and a tan belt, I complete my outfit. My make-up is light, and I add some gold hoop earrings and a gold bangle bracelet. It's simple yet classy and casual. After taking another look at myself in the mirror, I decide to make my way downstairs and help set up.

Once I get down the stairs, I see that Annabelle and Brooke are in a ruckus in order to get everything together in time. Walking into the kitchen, I decide to do my part. First, I pull out the cakes for the wedding from the freezer so they can defrost. I could see Annabelle and Brooke were working on the food, so I jump right in assisting. I smile to myself seeing the three men in the living room blowing up pink and white balloons. I am happy we are on a time crunch and we don't have time for small talk. It is bad enough every time I see Jackson, my face blushes with thoughts of him in my dream.

When the doorbell rings I notice the men scattering out the back door lightning fast. Smiling to myself at how fast they moved, I wasn't prepared to open the door to the brown haired girl that was all up on Jackson at the hoe down. It turns out her name is Savannah. I found out later the cute blonde with the fake rack is Cheyenne. I don't know why I thought that I wouldn't run into them again. This is a wedding week and they either had to know the bride or groom or be a plus one. Seeing how they hit on Jackson, the plus one obviously was off the table. I smile sweetly to both of them but don't purposefully make conversation.

For the most part, I serve the food and keep the place tidy, acting like the hostess instead of a bridesmaid. It wasn't until we were half way in the bridal shower that things got interesting.

I was bringing the punch bowl back into the dining room after refilling it, when I overheard Savannah.

"God, he's so sexy. When he kissed me last night, I swear the place could've burned down and I wouldn't have noticed. I can't wait till tonight if you know what I mean."

I didn't know who she was talking about at first until Annabelle made quick work of finding out.

"Who kissed you?" She asked. God, I love her and her questions.

"Jackson of course. That boy is fine." Savannah clarified.

That was all it took. I set the punch bowl down without spilling it and stormed out of the dining room. I had to get away before I lost it. I can't believe this. I thought about going upstairs but I knew Annabelle would come for me, so I decided to leave. I grabbed my keys off the front table and hopped into my car. I didn't know where I was going and I didn't care, I just knew I had to get out of there. Turning on the car, I backed out of the driveway and hauled ass until I was out of sight. It didn't take long for the tears to hit my eyes. I knew they would come. I just couldn't believe this was happening. I let Jackson in and he hurt me. I let him kiss me for goodness sake, and in return this is what happened. He played me! I actually thought maybe he likes me and he wants me. He said he smiles when I laugh, who does that? He said that he had wanted to kiss me for as long as he could remember. Was that a line? Did he say that to Savannah too? I could've actually sworn that he meant it, but as usual my Jackson radar failed me. I thought he liked me before and I was wrong, just like I am wrong now. I hate myself for letting my guard down and allowing myself to be hurt by him AGAIN! In attempts to drown out my thoughts, I decide to turn on the radio as loud as I can. Flipping through the stations for a song I can sing along to, I come across one that hits dead on. Joan Jet "I Hate Myself For Loving You". As if dedicating this song to Jackson on stage, I belt out the lyrics as loud as I can.

It wasn't until I heard the loud POP, and the car started swerving, that I was pulled from my own personal American Idol audition. Holding on to the wheel with everything I had, I was able to guide myself to safety on the side of the road. *SHIT!* Throwing my head back on the headrest, I sigh loudly. Of course this would happen. Opening the car door, I get out and find that I have a flat tire. *Great!* I am in the middle of nowhere with a freaking flat tire. Now what? I can't call Annabelle because it is in the middle of her bridal shower, and I don't want to disturb her. I was rude enough already by running out. I don't have Conner's number, nor Brooke and Nathan's, not to mention Jackson's. I am far from home, so other friends are out. I could call a tow truck, they change flat tires right? What the hell, doesn't hurt to find out. I don't carry cash on me, but most business allows you to pay with credit cards over the phone now.

I make my way to the car to retrieve my credit card and get it ready, when I realize I don't have my purse. My purse is sitting in my bedroom at the house. I have my cell, because it was in my pocket. And my keys were at the front door, but I have no purse, no money, no credit cards, and no ID. *CRAP!* Why does this stuff keep happening to me? It's like I am a cursed. Pacing back and forth several times, I come to the conclusion that I have two options. First: I could call Annabelle and have someone come help me, but that would ruin her party. Second: I could attempt to fix the flat tire myself.

Choosing option number two, I make my way to the trunk. There has to be directions right? Why did I not pay more attention to this when my father showed me growing up? *UGH.* I think I remember the basics, and there's always Google right? Making my way to the trunk, I move everything over, finding the spare tire and the jack. *I can do this!* Laughing to myself, I think this whole weekend is becoming one gigantic pep talk fuck up! As I pull out the jack and spare tire from the trunk, I find the thing-ma-jiggy, so I grab that too. I get the concepts. Jack the car up, taking the pressure off the tire. Take the lug nut things off using the thing-ma-jiggy to loosens the tire from tire holder, so you able to take the tires off. Replace with the spare tire and put the lug nut things back on. Tighten the lug nuts, using the thing-ma-jiggy. Then remove the jack and viola. You've changed the tire. *I can do this!* In attempts to make sure I am not forgetting any steps, I decide to check Google. Unfortunately, the wooded area doesn't seem to like the internet. I only get to the part about putting rocks under the other tires to prevent the car from moving, before the internet goes dead.

Well, good thing I at least got the part about securing the car. Knowing my luck I could see the car rolling down the hill, and me chasing it. Waving my hands in the air like it's going to come to an abrupt stop, just because I waved it down like a mad woman. No one needs to see that! I look around the wooded area and find several rocks. Deciding I want to make sure my chasing car scene doesn't pan out, I find twice as many rocks and place them in front of and behind each tire. I can never be too cautious with my luck.

Grabbing the jack, I place it under the car frame, next to the flat tire. I get two little pushes in before it won't move anymore. I try using my feet, and then my whole body, but nothing is budging it. Every time I attempt to make the jack move a little more, I wind up slipping and landing on the ground, up against the car, or on the tire. *Screw it!* I decide to move on. Hopefully my two little pushes were enough to take the pressure off the tire. I grab the thing-ma-jiggy and go to town on the lug nuts. They`re not budging either. *GOD!* Why do they make these things where you have to be the Hulk in order to get them to move? No wonder my mother used to tell me, "The way a woman changes a flat tire is to wear a black mini skirt and bend over." Except that wouldn't work here seeing as I am in the middle of nowhere and no one is driving by! *UGH...*

I try several more times before I begin cursing and beating the thing-ma-jiggy on the asphalt. After a few good blows to release my anger, I throw the thing-ma-jiggy on the ground and lean up against the car. I`m tired, I'm thirsty, I'm sweaty and hot and to top it off, I`m now covered in grease, brake dust, and dirt. No wonder I can never get a guy like Jackson to look at me twice. I`m not worth it! I can't even jack up a car and change a tire for goodness sake. Sitting down on the ground, I lean my back up against the car. Covering my face with my brake dusted hands, I begin to cry. After a few minutes have passed, I wipe my tears and decide to suck up my pride and call Annabelle.

# Chapter 13

## *What are you talking about*

Making the call was hard to do, having it go to voicemail officially sucked. I left a message explaining that I got a flat tire and where I was stranded. I also told her I was sorry for interrupting her bridal shower and running out on her like I did. Once I hung up, I put my forehead back to my knees, hugging my legs with my arms. I didn't know how long I was going to have to wait. Her party started at eleven and I ran out around noon. I called her and left a message an hour after I ran out. The party was supposed to last for two hours. I figure with people staying late to mingle, I should be picked up by two p.m. If not, I would call again. Looking down at my watch, which is now smothered in brake dust and grease, I see its five minutes till two. Screw it, it's close enough. Picking up the phone, I call Annabelle again.

She answers on the first ring.

"EMILY! Oh my god! I just got your voice mail. Are you okay? I`m so sorry, I didn't have my phone on me during the party!" She says frantically.

"I'm fine. Can you come and get me?"

"I called Conner. The guys are out that way grabbing a drink. He said they would come help you. Are you sure you're okay? You sounded like you were crying on the voicemail," Annabelle asks worriedly.

"I`m good, I was just upset about getting a flat tire and not being able to fix it. Hey, I think that's them, I'm going to let you go. See you soon." I say deceivingly. Hanging up the phone, I don't really see them but I didn't want to discuss why I was crying either. What do I say? The guy I have been in love with my entire life finally kisses me, and then he decides to kiss another girl the same night. Or, that I am pathetic and can`t change a tire. Throwing my head back against the car, I sigh loudly. *My life sucks!* Five minutes later, I glance up and see the white Ford Fusion pull up behind my car.

Jackson gets out and rushes over to me shouting, "Emily, are you okay?" Stopping in front of me, he reaches out to move a piece of hair from my face.

I jerk away from his hand quickly, snapping at him, "I`m fine."

Laced with concern, he asks, "You don't look fine. What the hell happened to you?"

Looking up at him, I gesture to the flat tire before saying heatedly, "I got a flat tire!"

"I can see that. I am asking about you?" He growls, waving his hands up and down in front of me.

I can see he is pissed and a little concerned, but why? I didn't go around kissing other girls or guys. Looking down at my outfit, I close my eyes. *Sweet Mercy!* I look hideous. I can't see my face or hair, but looking at my clothes I can see where I wiped my hands on my outfit. I also see where I have fallen multiple times with the marks on my jeans to prove it.

Looking up at him, I explain, "I tried to change the tire myself, but obviously I couldn't. I couldn't get the freaking jack to go up or the thing-ma-jiggy to turn the lug nuts."

It was then I hear the sound of three males laughing. Turning around, I see Conner and Nathan standing at the end of my Jetta. I was starting to think it couldn't get worse until Conner walks over and picks up the thing-ma-jiggy, asking, "What happened to this? Why is it way over here?"

*Oh sweet Jesus.* Well, might as well tell the truth. Rolling my eyes, I answer bluntly, "Well, I got a little pissed because I couldn't change the tire and after beating it on the ground, I kind of tossed it over to the side so I wouldn't have to look at it."

The three men burst into fits of laughter again. Nathan finally stops laughing long enough to ask, "So, you beat the lug nut wrench on the ground?" He says pointing to the thing-ma-jiggy, chuckling.

"Yes!" I admit.

Conner steps toward me laughing, "And when the lug wrench made you mad, you threw it away so you wouldn't have to look at it?"

"YES!" I say frustrated.

Jackson interrupts them and asks, "Baby, why do you look like you have been rolling in the dirt though?"

He called me baby. Normally I would be all mushy over this but after he kissed another girl, all it does is piss me off.

Exasperated I sigh loudly emphasizing, "BECAUSE. I. TRIED. TO. CHANGE. MY. TIRE."

Giving up on them, I storm off to the front of the car. Why must they make fun of me? I just want to cry again or hit something. I hear the muffles of the men talking, but I don't turn around. That is until I see the white Ford Fusion passing me. Looking over, I see Conner and Nathan in the car.

"What are you doing? Aren't you going to help me?" I say panicking. Holy crap they are leaving me!

"Calm down Emily. Jackson is changing your tire right now." Conner clarifies.

"We will see you at the house." With a short wave, Nathan and Conner drive off.

Glancing over, I see Jackson is jacking up the car. *Great!* I am being left alone with Mr. Playboy himself. Deciding he doesn't need any help, I turn and watch the Ford Fusion fade from my vision.

"Didn't mean to offend you babe." Jackson says sincerely.

What? Didn't mean to offend me? Is he talking about the kiss? He didn't offend me; he pissed me the hell off. He made me feel like chopped liver. Does he not get that? Does he think it is okay to kiss more than one girl at a time?

Turning toward him, I see he is diligently working on my tire. *God!* I know I am pissed off at him, but my mind absently notes how hot he looks changing my tire. Shaking the thoughts from my head, I reply firmly, "I`m not offended. If that is how you choose to do things, then so be it. But it's not the way I do them, so please leave me out of it."

"What are you talking about?" He says clearly confused.

"What do you mean what are you talking about?"

Standing up, he replies defensively, "Well, seeing how I was talking about how I didn't mean to offend you, by saying you looked like you rolled in dirt when I arrived. I'm guessing you are talking about something else."

"What?" *Oh No!* I thought we were talking about the kiss and he was talking about the car. *Shit!* How do I get out of this? What do I say?

"What did you think we were talking about Emily?"

"Nothing," I say quickly, trying to evade his question.

He takes a step toward me and I back up immediately.

"What the fuck?" He clips.

"Can we just get back to changing the tire?" I ask hesitantly.

"I will get back to changing the tire after you tell me what you were talking about. And why you are backing away from me?" He says with a hint of anger.

"Look I'm just tired and desperately need a shower. Can we please just get back to the tire, so we can go home?" I beg.

It`s true, I do need a shower. But more importantly, I am not about to discuss him kissing other females out here in the middle of the woods.

"Fine," He concedes. Turning around, he stalks back to the car and begins working on the tire.

I try not to look his way while he changes the tire. Because if I do, I find myself staring at him and the way his muscles flex when he moves. When I see him out of the corner of my eye throw the old tire in the trunk, I make my way to the driver side door.

"I drive," he demands.

"It's my car."

"I changed the flat. I`m a guy. I drive. It's what we do."

"I don't care, it's my car!" I snap.

Moving in front of the driver side door, he halts my attempt at opening it up.

*What the hell!*

"Babe, not saying it again. Hand over the keys."

Standing with my mouth wide open, I can't believe him. How dare he!

"I can wait all day, but I think you said you were tired and wanted a shower," He says nonchalantly.

He's serious. *UGH*. Shoving the keys in his chest, I storm off to the passenger door. I'm not going to fight with him. I just want to go home and get far away from him. If that means he drives my old Jetta to make it happen, fine by me. Opening up the passenger side door, I plant my ass in the seat. Crossing my arms on my chest, I look out my window, sighing loudly. He can drive, but that doesn't mean I have to make conversation with him.

Climbing in the car, he starts it up, when "Toxic" by Britney Spears comes blaring thru the speakers.

"Jesus!" He mutters, turning off the radio.

"Hey! My car. My radio. You got your way with driving, but you don't get the radio too!" I say snippily turning the radio on again.

"I'm not listening to that shit."

"You don't have a choice!" I snap, narrowing my eyes at him.

He stares at me for a second, before looking back out the front windshield. Putting the car in drive, he pulls out onto the road. I do my best to avoid him, but I can't help but notice that he doesn't seem to have a speck of dirt on him after changing the tire. How does that happen?

We are about a mile away from the turn that leads to the house, when he pulls off on the side of the road.

"What are you doing?" I ask curiously.

Putting the car in park, he turns in his seat, looking up at me, "We are going to talk."

"No, I'm good," I say matter of factly.

"Well, I'm not driving us the rest of the way until we do. Now, what were you talking about earlier? What do I choose to do, that I can leave you out of?"

Closing my eyes, I plead, "Please, just drive us back to the house Jackson."

"Not going to happen, now talk." He demands

Opening my eyes, I look up at him and beg softly, "Jackson please."

"I have wanted to hear you say those words to me for a long time babe, just not like this," He confesses.

"You can't say stuff like that to me." I whisper.

"Why not?" He asks nonchalantly.

"Why not?" *UGH!*

"Yeah, Emily, why?" He pushes.

"Because, I'm not Savannah!" I shout.

"What the fuck?" He clips, looking confused.

"I know."

"You know what?" He asks.

"I know that last night when you kissed me, you kissed her too." Looking away, I find myself picking at my fingernails in my lap. "I can't do that. If that's how you choose to do things, that's fine. But I can't do that."

"That's why you jerked away from me? When I walked up to you at the car, you jerked away."

I can't bring myself to answer, so I nod in agreement.

"Emily, look at me."

Doing as he says, I turn my head and look up at him.

"I didn't kiss her, she kissed me," he explains.

Rolling my eyes, he continues.

"I know you don't believe me when I say that, but it's true. She caught me off guard last night. I assure you Emily, I am not into her," he says lifting his hand and touching my cheek. "What I said was true last night. I have waited a long time to kiss you. Now that I have, you better believe I have no intention of letting you slip away from me again."

Closing my eyes, I bite my lip. I don't know what to say. I feel his lips brush my forehead before he pulls back, dropping his hand from my cheek. With that, he puts the car in drive and pulls back out onto the road heading toward the house.

# Chapter 14

## *Killer red dress*

We didn't speak after that. Instead, I sat in silence looking out the window with my thoughts. Do I believe him about kissing Savannah? Did he honestly mean what he said about our kiss last night? What does he mean, not letting me slip away? By the time we pull up to the house, it's almost three p.m. I still need to cover the cakes with fondant before the rehearsal at seven. Looking down at my clothes, I realize I need to change before I attempt to do anything. I decide to also take a quick shower, washing off the dirt and grease. When the car comes to a complete stop, I grab the handle opening the door.

Jackson halts my attempts at fleeing when he speaks, "Emily I know you need time, but what I said is true and I meant every word."

Not knowing what else to say, I continue to stare at the door replying, "Thank you for changing my tire."

Getting out of the car I hear him announce, "Anything for you babe."

With that, I make my way into the house and up the stairs before anyone can approach me. Once I am in my room, I grab my shower bag and begin to make my way to the bathroom. Annabelle stops me at our bedroom door, "So glad your back sweetie." Looking at me up and down, she finishes. "You look a mess. Did you leave any dirt on the car?"

"Not funny. Look, I just want to take a quick shower and then I really need to get started on the cakes. Can we finish this conversation later?"

"Yeah, later." She says before making her way downstairs.

Closing the door to the bathroom, I take the quickest shower known to man. Hopping out, I run to my bedroom throwing on a pair of faded blue jeans that have a rip in the knee with a grey tank top. I throw on a big oval neck white shirt that says "true" on it in grey, and finish off my outfit with my blue converses. Brushing my hair, I leave it to dry naturally. With no makeup and no jewelry, I make my way downstairs to start on the cakes.

Once I am in the kitchen I notice a plate on the island with a note beside it. Picking up the note, I read it:

*Emily, we are out in the barn setting up for the reception. Thought you might be hungry after your adventurous day.*
*Don't forget rehearsal is at seven p.m. We will run thru the ceremony here and then we are meeting everyone for dinner in town. Just holler if you need any help making the cakes.*
*Love, Annabelle*
*PS: I haven't forgotten about our later conversation*

Putting the note down, I grab a slice of pizza off the plate and dig in. She was right, I am starving. After I woof down the pizza, I grab all my supplies. At least I remembered to pull out the cakes prior to the bridal shower. Checking them, I see they are still a little frozen but workable. Looking at my watch, I see it is three thirty p.m. I need to start getting ready at six p.m., so I set the timer on my phone and turn on my music. Being mindful that I can't get lost in the music and make a fool of myself again, I settle for Saving Abel "Addicted".

Laying the cakes out, I start to work on leveling them. Once they are all leveled, I spread a quick layer of icing on top to start soaking in. Spreading out a layer of flour on the counter to work on, I pull out the fondant. While beating the fondant to make it softer, I hear the music change to Christina Aguilera`s, "Genie in a bottle".

Every time I hear this song I think back to when I was sixteen and in Jackson's pickup truck. He was driving us to meet up with friends and this song came on. My mind being in the gutter I was singing the song out loud and had changed the words to say "come and lick me up" instead of "come and let me out". He had caught this and I remember he turned off the radio and immediately said, "What did you just say?" Embarrassed, I couldn't think and told him exactly what I said. He laughed and said "that's not how the song goes," and I remember saying "I know." That was the longest and quietest trip ever. Thinking back I can't help but be embarrassed and laugh at my own stupidity. I really need to learn to think quickly on my feet.

Smiling, I spread out the fondant and prime it for the cake. The music changes over to Stroke 9 "Do It Again," when I notice Jackson walking in the kitchen. Looking up at him, I see his lips curve up at the sides.

"Hi," I say nervously.

"Hey babe," he replies sweetly.

Turning my head back to the fondant, I continue working. I see him out of the corner of my eye coming closer to me, and then he stops when he is right next to me. Hips to the counter, he reaches out and brushes a piece of hair behind my ear. Twisting my head, I look up at him and find his gaze sweeping me up and down.

Then speaking softly, like if he is talking to himself, he says, "So beautiful even without the makeup."

I notice his eyes drop to my mouth and turn darker. Unconsciously, I lick my lips. When he spoke, his voice dipped lower sending a pleasant tingly sensation down to my nether regions and I cannot lie, my nipples hardened instantly. "Keep looking at me like that and I won't be able to give you the time you need."

With that, he drops his hand from my hair and takes a step toward the island. Grabbing the last slice of pizza off my plate, he leaves the kitchen. I decide not to think about it. Picking up the fondant, I spread it over the cake.

Once the fondant is in place over the big bottom cake, I work on the next two. I get them covered, smoothed out, and stacked on top of each other when the timer goes off. I quickly clean up and decide to finish up tomorrow. They don't have perfect lines but I can hide that with the flowers. Making my way upstairs, I head toward my bedroom. I know the rehearsal is fancy, so I`m thrilled I brought my red dress. It`s killer. It is a one-shoulder, form fitting dress that pulls together a little at the waist on one side. To be honest, if I gained five pounds I wouldn't be able to fit in it, it is that tight. It stops just below the knee and has a slit up the back to allow you to walk. I pair it with diamond tear drop earrings and a double layer diamond necklace that lays loosely on the dress. Not having a pair of red heals that match perfectly; I decide to go with a nude color. I straighten out my hair and put on light makeup. Looking in the mirror, I smile to myself. *Oh yeah!* This will make Jackson`s blood boil. So happy I brought this dress!

"Emily! It's time to get this started, come on!" I hear Brooke shouting from downstairs.

"Coming!" I yell back at her. Grabbing my purse, I switch it out for my nude clutch purse that matches my shoes, before making my way downstairs.

When I hit the bottom of the stairs, I hear Brooke announce, "Wow! You look hot as hell. I swear if I wasn't happily married I would be considering the other side looking at you."

Blushing I mutter, "Thanks."

We head out the back door behind the house where tomorrow`s ceremony will take place.

Annabelle has decided to do an outdoor wedding. Nothing is set up yet, except a plain arch sitting in the middle of the backyard. Looking at it now, I don't see how it will all be done in time but I know Annabelle, aka Bridezilla has her ways. We find everyone huddled in a circle next to the arch. Brooke and I make our way over when I see Jackson. *Holy Smokes!* He looks amazing. He`s wearing black slacks that hug his thighs and a dark grey button down collared shirt. I just want to pounce on him. Looking at the ground, I attempt to stop myself from staring at him. I need to focus on walking or else I'm going to trip and probably rip my dress.

Once we are all standing in a circle, the old guy I assume is the priest starts to explain how the wedding will work. The priest advises us that there will be rows of chairs on both sides of the arch that we will make our way through. Once we reach the arch, we will line up on the left side for the remainder of the ceremony. Everything after that becomes one big blur until Conner shouts, "Limos here, let's eat!" Enthusiastically Nathan says, "That's what I'm talking about."

With that we start walking toward the limo and of course, I trip. I knew it was coming. I swear to this day, the Ms. Congeniality movie was made to mock me.
I throw my hands out to catch myself, but I never make it to the ground. I am halted by a pair of arms wrapped around my waist. Looking down at the arms around me, I hear his soft voice in my ear and my breath catches. "Easy love, I would hate for you to ruin this dress." Did he just call me love? I thought babe was good, but love is so much better.

Standing up tall, I try not to focus on the warmth of his arms around me or how good he feels.

"Thanks. Heels on an uneven surface get me every time," I try to explain.

Wiggling free of his arms, I make my way toward the limo. In an attempt not to embarrass myself again, I walk with extreme caution. I notice that he is not even two steps behind me the entire time. I hope this is just a coincidence and not that he is waiting to catch me again. You would think I would be used to this, seeing how I am the proverbial klutz, yet, I`m not. I am thankful though, when I make it to the limo without tripping again.

# Chapter 15

## *Not again*

Climbing into the limo, I immediately regret the red dress. It is halting my movements way too much. How am I going to be able to drink in this thing? I sit down next to Annabelle and Jackson sits down on the other side of me. His leg is pressed up against mine and the closeness is giving me a warm feeling in all the right places. Thankfully, Annabelle chooses that moment to interrupt my thoughts.

"So Emily, I do think it is time for that later conversation?" She says.

Dear lord, if she wasn't my best friend I would kill her. Feeling the blush creep up my cheeks, I attempt to nip the conversation as fast as I can. Blurting quickly I respond, "Not much to say. I tried to change my tire and kept falling instead. It's like you have to be some kind of hot macho man in order to change it."

Realizing what I just said, I clamp my mouth shut. Maybe he didn't hear me. *Fat chance!*

Leaning over towards me, he puts his hand on my leg, and whispers in my ear, "You think I'm a hot macho man?"

"No!" I lie.

Who am I kidding with that quick reply, I won`t fool anyone. I can tell I am right, when I hear Jackson laugh. I choose that time to look up at him, and he flashes me a heart stopping smile.

Annabelle interrupts, "Okay. Well, you never told me why you ran out of my bridal shower like someone had just told you they ran over your dog. Not to mention, when you left the voicemail you seemed to be crying."

*Oh lord*! I notice Jackson`s whole body tense next to me before he removes his hand off my leg. I feel the loss of his hand immediately. Sighing, I decide I have to do damage control. Glaring at Annabelle, I speak in a firm tone. "It was nothing. Someone, not going to name names, said something and I took it the wrong way. It turned out to be a big misunderstanding. It's all good now. So let's just drop it, okay."

"Okay," Annabelle agrees.

I see Jackson relax a little, but his hand never comes back to my leg.

I'm happy when we pull up to the restaurant, because I am more than ready to get out of the limo. Not to mention, I have got to pee. I make my way out the limo door and start walking toward the restaurant when a hand comes to my arm, stopping me. Looking up, I see that it's Jackson.

"One minute!" He demands.

"Sure," I say nervously.

Not dropping his hand from my arm, he leads me over to the side of the building.

"I didn't mean to hurt you or make you cry," he says honestly.

"I wasn't crying over you." I shoot back. Denial, it can't hurt. Plus I don't want him to know that I'm still secretly in love with him and he has that much power over me.

"Okay babe. We good?"

"Yeah," I assure him.

Pulling me into his body, he gives me a hug while placing a kiss in my hair.

"If I haven't told you yet, you look breathtaking," he states to my hair.

Taking in a deep breath, I blurt, "So do you, and you smell yummy too."

Chuckling, he pulls me closer, his arms tightening around me.

"Glad to have you back babe. Now let`s go eat. I`m starving." With that he pulls away, but takes my hand leading me toward the front of the building.

We walk inside the restaurant, hand in hand. My mind in awe, he called me breathtaking. I notice everyone sitting at the table and catch Brooke and Annabelle looking at us, then at our conjoined hands. Shaking my head back and forth, I attempt to warn them not to go there. Before we reach the table, I stop and Jackson looks back at me. I see the curiosity in his eyes so I explain, "Restroom."

Dropping my hand he says, "I'll meet you at the table." Then he proceeds to join our group and sit down.

I make my way to the bathroom and do my business. I use this time to devise a game plan. I decide that I'm just going to go with the flow. What happens, happens. My heart is already out there on the tight rope, seeing how my earlier crying fit gives confirmation of that. I can't protect what is already taken, so I decide to just let it ride. I still don't know if he cared for me back then, or why he didn't want me. He says he isn't letting me slip away again. Does that mean he purposely let me slip away before? I just have to proceed with extreme caution. Washing my hands, I look at myself in the mirror. *I can do this!* After a quick swipe of my lip gloss, I exit the bathroom.

Arriving at the table, I see the only available chair is next to Jackson. I wonder if he did that on purpose. I also note the chair is right up against his. Sitting down, I scoot closer to the table. It doesn't go unnoticed that Jackson has his arm along the back of my chair, as soon as I get settled. Smiling to myself, I try not to make a big deal out of it.

Conversation during dinner was intriguing to say the least. I laughed so hard several times that I thought I had ripped my dress. Mix in the numerous hefty glasses of wine I consumed and to say I was good to go was an understatement. I found myself leaning into Jackson`s side every once in a while. Not to mention his thumb would come up and brush the back of my arm, sending tingles all over my body. With his leg pressed up against mine and the smell of his cologne, I found myself loosing concentration at the table more than once. Especially when I would look up at him and he would smile at me, making me feel all warm and fuzzy.

When dinner ended, we made our way back to the limo. I couldn't help but notice that Jackson kept some kind of touch on me at all times. Whether it was walking out of the restaurant with his hand at the small of my back, guiding me, or sitting next to me in the limo on the way home with his arm over my shoulders and his thumb rubbing circles on my arm. I have to say, I loved it. It made me feel wanted and needed. Most importantly it was Jackson touching me. I have wanted this for as long as I could remember.

When we arrived at the house we all climbed out of the limo, and Jackson reached for my hand. I took it without thinking and let him guide me upstairs. I noticed Annabelle and Conner head off to the living room while Brooke and Nathan were already in their bedroom.

I knew at this moment, all I wanted was his lips on mine and the feel of his hands all over my body. At the top of the stairs, I took control, leading him to my bedroom door. I was done playing games. I wanted him. Pulling him into my room, I turned around to click the lock with my left hand. Slowly I turn back to face him, and see his eyebrows rise. Biting my lip, I give a slight tug of our conjoined hands and he steps toward me. I drop his hand and reach for his shirt, pulling him to me until his body is pressed up against mine. Tilting his head down, I notice his lips twitch. He must find me amusing trying to seduce him. *Oh well.* I want this to bad to turn back now.

Letting go of his shirt, I slide my hands slowly up his chest. Feeling every indentation of his heavenly sculpted chest and broad shoulders, I wrap my arms around his neck. He places his hands on my waist, moving them around to my back and my breathing picks up. This is it. Tipping my head back, he presses his lips to mine. His tongue enters my mouth, stroking every inch. I moan, pressing my body into his further. His right hand slides up my back, into my hair. While the other slides over my butt, pushing my hips into his. I can feel his hardness at my belly, causing a moan to escape my mouth. Lifting my hands into his hair, I bury them. He pulls his lips back, sucking on my bottom lip. The feel of his chest, his arms around me, his lips on me, I can't concentrate on anything except dropping my panties and hiking up my skirt.

Breaking our kiss, he starts traveling his lips slowly up my jaw to my ear.

Flicking my earlobe with his tongue, he blows a soft breath on my ear. Gripping his hair, I mutter, "I want you Jax."

I hear him groan while he squeezes his arms around me.

Pulling his head back, he brings his warm lust filled eyes to mine, speaking in a gravelly voice, "Trust me, I want you too. But not when you have been drinking."

What?? Nooooo...

"I'm completely sober! I swear!" Oh god, don't leave me hanging. I might self-combust here.

"I saw you down a whole bottle of wine, babe. When I am inside of you, I want you to remember and feel every moment of it."

"I will, trust me. I will!" I assure him. I know I sound desperate, but I don't care at this point.

Chuckling softly, he leans toward me, brushing his lips to mine once more, before he pulls back completely.

I teeter there for a second. He's going to leave me hanging... AGAIN! What the fuck? I need to work on my seduction skills. *Jesus!* Either that, or go buy a vibrator. How could he do this to me again?

"You are an asshole." I blurt out. Okay it might be rude, but so is leaving a girl high and dry.

Reaching up, he grabs my cheek brushing his thumb across my bottom lip. "I know, I`m going to hate myself as soon as I walk out that door, but it's the right thing to do," he says hesitating for a second. "I want to do this right. And if that means taking it slow, that is what I am going to do."

Then dropping his hand from my cheek, he unlocks the door and walks out calling, "Night babe."

"Screw you Jackson!" I yell, slamming the door shut.

# Chapter 16

## *What was that*

After slamming the door, I get ready for bed. I contemplate for a minute about finishing myself off. The only reason I don't, is with my luck, someone would come barging in and catch me mid act. Settling for my light blue satin baby doll, I call it a night and climb into bed.

Annabelle knocks on the door shortly after, before popping her head in. "Why did you knock?" I ask curiously. "I didn't want to interrupt you and Jackson doing the nasty. So, did you?" She asks sitting on the edge of my bed. Her hands are folded together like I'm about to tell her the biggest secret ever. Frustrated, I let out an exasperated sigh and decide to tell her the truth. Maybe she can tell me what I am doing wrong. I have never had a guy besides Jackson; flat out refuse me like that. It's making me feel off my game.

"He wouldn't. And believe me, I tried. I did everything except stand up naked in front of him. And I would've done that if I knew it wouldn't take too long to get undressed."

"What do you mean he wouldn't? Like he couldn't?" She asks curiously.

"No, I felt that so at least I know I turn him on. But he wouldn't. He didn't want to take me when I was drunk."

"You aren't drunk though."

"I know! I told him that! He didn't believe me." I say exasperated.

"So he just left?" She asks curiously.

"Yeah, but he did sprout some nonsense about wanting to do it right and take it slow. I'm just glad I caught myself before I blurted that I wanted it hard and fast."

We both laugh for a minute.

"Yeah, that would've been bad, but I would've loved to see his facial expression."

"Me too," I agree smiling.

"Maybe he really wants to do right by you since it went to shit the first time," Annabelle says thinking for a minute

while patting my leg with her hand.
"The way he looked at you tonight, not
to mention how he was always touching
you, makes me think he really does like
you Emily."

Smiling I respond, "Maybe, but it
wouldn't hurt to bend a girl over every
once in a while either."

"No, no it wouldn't," she says laughing.
"But Em, maybe taking it slow is a good
idea. Go with his flow and see where it
takes you. Try for once not to make the
first move. Maybe he is gun shy or old
fashioned and believes it needs to be
him and not you."

"You have a good point, and I will.
Now, let's get some sleep. You have a
big day tomorrow!"

"I KNOW! I can't wait!" Annabelle
squeals with delight.

   We both settle down and go to sleep
for the night. My thoughts are on
Jackson and I'm sure Annabelle`s are on
her impending wedding nuptials
tomorrow.

I hear a crash that jolts me awake from a deep sleep. I sit up rubbing my eyes when I hear another loud crash. My hands shoot to my mouth. *Oh shit!* Is someone breaking in? We are in the middle of the freaking woods for crying out loud. I look around and see Annabelle is doing the same as me. Looking at the clock, I note the time is three a.m.

"What do we do?" I whisper to Annabelle and see her shrug her shoulders. We hear a creak of the floor board outside our room. I can actually hear my heart pounding in my chest. Are they coming to get us? Why the hell didn't Jackson just stay with me tonight? Everyone knows the cute people die first. I have seen enough scary movies to know, that it has got to be a fact. I also know my ass is not going down stairs to find the cause of the noise. That is like asking to get killed. I try to remember anything I ever learned in self-defense class. Nope, nothing comes to mind. *Damn!* That was a waste of money.

Annabelle runs over to me and we sit together in my bed holding hands.

"Do you think the men know?" She whispers.

"I don't know how they couldn't hear that crash."

"What if they didn't?" Annabelle asks nervously.

"I'm not going out there," I state firmly.

"Me neither," she agrees.

CRASH! BANG!

Then the door swings open and we both scream bloody murder.

"SHUSH, it's just me," Jackson says.

*Oh thank heavens!*

"Are you girls okay?" He asks.

We both nod our heads up and down. Never in my life have I wanted to jump in the arms of a man as bad as I do right now.

"Stay here!" He orders.

"You're leaving? You can't leave! I have watched enough of those scary movies to know that we will die if you leave. You can't leave us!" I demand.

Shifting his head to the side, I see him flash me a smile, "I will be back. Stay here. Lock the door and only open it when I tell you to."

"Are you serious?" I say anxiously.

"Yes, if it will make you feel better grab something to use just in case someone comes to the door."

"Like what, the lamp?" I snap.

"Babe, I'll be back. You will be fine, I promise," he replies calmly.

CRASH! Then I hear the sound of a grunt and then a thump.

I look past Jackson and see Nathan ushering in Brooke. She is as pale as a ghost.

"You ready?" Jackson says.

"Yeah, where is Conner?" Nathan asks.

"Downstairs," Jackson says, and Annabelle gasps.

"Have you called 911?" Nathan questions.

"Conner did before he went downstairs." Nathan nods in approval.

"Stay here. Lock the door," Nathan says, shutting the door behind him.

Brooke joins us on my bed and we all hold hands. We hear grunting and a thud every once in a while but other than that it's quiet.

Annabelle is the first to speak, "Do you think Conner is okay?"

"I`m sure he is," I say to reassure her.

"You are a blabbermouth when you are scared Emily," Brooke interjects, making us all laugh.

We sit in silence for what seems like forever but when I look down at the clock, it has only been two minutes. *Oh No!* Then it dawns on me, we didn't lock the door. I get up and Annabelle and Brooke grab my arm.

"Where are you going?" Brooke inquires.

"We didn't lock the door?" I retort.

"Crap!" Annabelle says as they both let go of my arm, so I can walk to the door.

# Chapter 17

### *You left me*


As soon as I get close enough to the door that I can bend over and barely reach the knob to turn it, it flings open. I jump back screaming and attempt to turn midair in order to run back to the bed when an arm wraps around my waist. I fight against the arm holding me to get away. It has got to be whoever broke in. Probably an axe murderer! *Crap!* I'm going to die tonight! I swing my hand back trying to clock the person in the head when I hear Jackson say, "Calm down woman."

At the sound of his voice, I relax into his arms. He takes my weight, pulling me into him.

Annabelle stutters,

"Wh…Where's….Conner?"

"He's downstairs with Nathan. They are fine. They are waiting on the cops to show."

"Can we go downstairs?" Brooke asks nervously.

"Yes. Be careful, there is quite a mess down there though."

Annabelle and Brooke nod, before they leave out the room quickly to find their men.

I turn around in Jackson's arms, wrapping mine around his waist. My face lands in his chest and I melt fully into him. His right hand comes to my head, stroking my hair back from my face.

"I told you I would be back, babe."

"You shouldn't have left me in the first place." I snap.

"I had to help them. I promised I would come back and I did."

He had a point, but I surely wasn't going to tell him that. Realizing he was downstairs doing whatever they did down there, I push back from him, moving my hands over his shirt and down his arms, chest and abdomen. Smiling he asks, "What are you doing?"

"Making sure you aren't bleeding or anything."

Pulling me back into his chest, he laughs, "I`m fine babe, but I did almost get clobbered in the head by a sexy mad woman."

"Real funny Jax. You could've been hurt."

"But I wasn't so stop worrying. It's over now," he confirms.

We listen as the siren`s pull up to the house.

"Should we go down there?" I say hesitantly, biting my lip.

"Yeah," He says pulling back. Looking at me up and down he clips, "What the hell are you wearing?"

"Pajamas," I say, slightly confused by his question.

"Jesus!" He says throwing his head back, "You are killing me babe. Do you have a robe or something?"

"No. Why?" I ask innocently.

"You need to put something else on. You aren't going out there in that." He says pointing to my baby doll nightgown.

Rolling my eyes, I grab a big oversized t shirt and put it on.

He growls, "Not much better babe."
"Get over it, I didn't pack long sleeve footed pajamas or a mumu Jax."

Making our way downstairs, I see the front table is smashed on the floor. My body goes tight at the sudden realization of what probably happened down here. Jackson puts his arm around my shoulder, pulling me into his side. "You okay babe."
"Yeah," I say wrapping my arms around his waist.

We stay in this position as we walk into the living room where everyone is standing. My front is almost fully plastered to his side, but I don't care. I feel safe in his arms. I take note that the couch is moved and the end table is broken, along with the lamp that was on it. The coffee table is now a bunch of broken wooden pieces on the floor. Conner is across the room, holding Annabelle in almost the same position that Jax is holding me. I see Nathan in the kitchen with Brooke in his arms. Her back is fully plastered to his front and his arms are around her shoulders, holding her close. The men spend the next twenty minutes giving their statements to the cops. Turns out someone had escaped from the prison a couple miles away and tried to seek refuge here. Thankfully, there were three men here against one escapee.

After the men try to do a make shift job of shutting the door to make sure no one can open it again, we head upstairs. Watching Annabelle go with Conner to his room, I realize I don't want to be alone tonight. After all that happened, I'm to chicken shit to be by myself. How do I ask him? Will he tell me no? If he does, what am I going to do? Deciding to bite the bullet, I let him have it.

Biting my lip, I stop walking and look up into Jackson`s eyes.

"Jax," I say hesitantly.

At the sound of me calling his name, he stops walking. Tilting his head down, he lifts his hand and brushes the hair away from my face, "Yeah, babe."

Closing my eyes, I muster up all the courage I can. "Um…Okay…Look, I know you wanted to take it slow and all,

pg. 167

and that's fine. But I…I just can't be alone tonight," I blurt.

"Babe," he says softly.

"Please Jax. We don't have to do anything, but I would be lying if I said what happened tonight didn't scare the shit out of me and I…. I just feel safe with you. Okay?" I say taking a deep breath.

"I wouldn't want it any other way," he assures me, pulling me into his arms.

We stand like this for a few minutes, before he pulls away from me. Taking my hand, he guides me into my bedroom. Once inside I take off my oversized t shirt and climb into my bed. I watch as he pulls off his shirt revealing his edible chest. Biting my lip, I close my eyes. I can't think like this. He is here to keep me safe, not for me to be thinking of all the things I want to do to him. How I want to push him down on the bed and climb on top. Maybe bite his nipples. *Yum!* Honestly, I really wouldn't mind nibbling a lot of things on him if I could get the chance. Shaking my head to rid my thoughts, I open my eyes to see he is standing in front of me. Reaching out, I grab ahold to his hand, pulling him toward me.

"We should get some sleep," he says. Agreeing with him, I nod my head.

"You okay?" He asks.

"Lay with me?" I ask hesitantly.

He looks at the bed before bringing his eyes back at me. I can tell he is thinking about it. Kicking off his shoes, he unzips his pants and lets them fall to the floor.

"Lay down!" he demands.

Climbing into the bed behind me, he pulls the covers over us. We are both on our sides, facing each other. My hands are under my head like I am praying, while he has his left hand under his head with the right one on my waist.

"Jackson?"

"Yeah, babe."

"Can I ask you something?" I say hesitantly.

"You can ask me anything," he says reassuringly.

I don't say anything for a while. I know I am chickening out. What if he gets mad at me? What if I don't like his answer? I don't think I can do this.

"Spit it out Emily."

"Um…" I hesitate.

"Emily."

"What`s your tattoo of?" I blurt.

"It`s a Chinese symbol meaning Inner Strength," he explains.

"Oh! That`s cool." I never would`ve guessed that.

"That`s not what you wanted to ask, so spit it out," he says in a serious tone.

Looking up at him I decide all or nothing. I have wanted answers and the only way to get them is to ask. Taking a deep breath, I let it all hang out.

"Okay… I just…Do you remember when we were younger and I…I asked you…"

"Yeah, I remember," he confirms.

"You do?" I ask, and he nods in agreement.

"I thought you liked me," I say uncertainly.

"I did," he assures me.

"But you said I was too young for you."

"You were," he admits. I guess he can tell it's not what I wanted to hear, so he continues. "You were seventeen and I was over eighteen. If anything would have happened between us I could`ve gotten in a lot of trouble. Not just with the law, but with my career. I was just starting out in the Navy and they frown on things like that. I couldn't risk it. I wanted to, but I couldn't."

"I thought it was because you just didn't want me," I confess.

Using his hand at my waist, he pulls me closer to him, "It wasn't that I didn't want you. It was never that. You are the prettiest girl I have ever laid eyes on. If I would`ve known the last time you would speak to me was that night in the car, I would`ve handled it differently. Hell, I would've stopped you all together."

"Why? If you wanted me, why would you have stopped me?" I ask confused.

"Because if you would`ve saved that exact conversation for another several months, then things could've happened a lot differently," he explains.

I nod, unsure of what to say.

"I came back for you," he says.
"When you graduated nursing school, I looked you up and came by your house. You weren't home."

"I remember my neighbor mentioning a really hot guy stopping by my house. I thought she was just crazy and seeing things." I say grinning.

"You said you were scared of me at the hoe down, why is that?" He pushes changing the subject.

Closing my eyes I whisper, "I`m afraid that you will turn me down again, or that you won't want me the way I want you."

He removes his hand at my waist bringing it up to my neck, "Emily look at me."

Opening my eyes, I do as he says.

"I have no intentions of leaving you and I can assure you that I want you," he says, brushing his lips to mine quickly before pulling back. "Now sleep, we have a big day tomorrow."

"Right," I say yawning.

I decide to turn my backside to him. There is no way that I am going to be able to sleep when all I have to do is open my eyes and see his glorious body in front of me. Twisting around, I push my butt up into his groin and hear him grunt under his breath. Putting his arm around my waist, he pulls my body against his. I fall fast asleep in his arms in a matter of minutes.

## Chapter 18

### *Not again*

Waking up with Jackson's arms around me is a dream come true. Feeling his bare chest pressed up against my back is unbelievably amazing.

"Emily," he whispers softly in my ear. Snuggling deeper into him I feel his right hand sliding up my waist. It didn't help that my baby doll night gown rode up through the night and was now sitting just under my breast, revealing my lace underwear.

"Hum," was all I could respond.

Rolling to my back, he remains on his side partially towering over me. His hand at my waist skims my belly when I turn, landing on my side. Up on his elbow, his left hand sifts through my hair. Opening my eyes, I look up at him to find his eyes are warm and filled with lust. Leaning down, he presses his lips softly against mine. My hands have a mind of their own. One dives into his hair, while the other moves around his waist, pulling my body deeper into his.

I deepen the kiss while running my left hand up his back. Groaning, he rolls until he is fully on top of me. Lifting my legs, I wrap them around his waist. He breaks our kiss, but only to start trailing his lips from my neck, down my chest. His hand moves up and under my night gown, skimming the underside of my breast. I press my chest into him, giving him the signal that I wanted more. Okay, the move was more like please God keep going, don't you dare stop or I will kill you, but, he didn't need to know that.

Pulling my nightgown up and over my head, he reveals my breasts. Bending his head, he takes my right breast in his mouth. He tugs on my nipple with his teeth, before doing a delicious swirl with his tongue. I thought I was going to orgasm just from his touch and the feel of his mouth on me. Dragging my nails along his back, I moan out loud. He releases my nipple, moving to my other breast. His hand slides down to the top of my panties where he traces the waistband, teasing me. Pushing my hips to meet his, I plead with him, "Please." It was barely audible even to my own ears, but I know he heard me. My heart is racing and I realize I am begging, but I don't care. I have wanted to do this with Jackson for as long as I can remember.

At my plea, he stops his delicious assault with my breast and looks up at me. Pressing his hips into mine, I feel his hardness. *Oh sweet Jesus that feels nice!* Biting my lip, I attempt to halt the groan escaping my mouth. Bringing his head down, he kisses me on the lips again. This time the kiss is hard and rough, filled with passion. I melt further into him and feel his hand slide under the waistband of my panties, sending a shiver over my body. I didn't care if he could feel it. Sliding both my hands down into his boxer briefs, I dig my nails into his ass pushing him to me. I feel his finger slide back and forth between my wet folds. *Oh God!* "You're soaking wet babe," he growls approvingly. Bending his head he starts traveling kisses down my navel to my panties. His finger drags up my folds until they come to my clit, where he presses in a circular motion.

Whimpering out loud, I could tell it wasn't going to take much more.

Bending his head, he kisses me over my panties.

KNOCK KNOCK KNOCK.

"OH HELL NO!" I shout. "Ignore it, keep going!"

KNOCK KNOCK KNOCK

Resting his forehead on my belly, Jackson lets out a frustrated sigh.

"Time to get up guys, lots to do today!" Annabelle shouts from the other side of the door.

Closing my eyes, I bitterly declare, "I hate her right now."

Kissing my belly, Jackson sits up stating, "We will finish this later babe, I promise."

With that he bends his head, swiftly planting a kiss on my lips before getting up off the bed.

I continue to lay there plotting my revenge against Annabelle. Why does this keep happening to me? Jackson tugs on his pants, before putting on his shoes. Pulling his shirt over his head, he walks to the door. Turning around to look at me one more time, he smiles, "I don't mind this view babe, but I`d prefer if you didn't show it to everyone else when I open the door."

Narrowing my eyes at him, I sit up and put my night gown on. Throwing my legs to the side of the bed, I hear him mumble, "So gorgeous," as he opens the door and walks out.

There is a lot to do today before the wedding, not to mention the cleanup downstairs. I know I have to go grab the flowers and finish up the cakes. The wedding is at five p.m. tonight. Annabelle was specific on wanting the sun setting for her wedding pictures. I have to admit, it does sound romantic. Looking at the clock I see that it is eight a.m. Brooke has scheduled us girls with time at the spa to get our hair and nails done. We were given specific instructions to be showered and ready at one p.m. in order to leave for the spa.

This way, when we get home, all we have to do is get dressed for the wedding. The men I was told are being left with picture diagrams and specific instructions for the different wedding vendors. They are going to set up the barn for the reception while we go to the spa, as well as help set up for the ceremony.

I decide to go ahead and get dressed for the day. Going with a casual outfit, I put on a tan, halter back tank top with my teal short shorts. Throwing my hair in a high pony tail, I put on my teal flip flops that wrap around my feet. I top off my outfit with my teal scoop neck triple banded necklace and my teal hoop style earrings. I apply light makeup and change my purse back over to my brown Coach purse. Throwing on my brown belt, I walk to the bedroom door.

Making my way downstairs, I find everyone is cleaning up the mess from last night's encounter. The men are picking up the left over remains of the broken tables, and taking them outside. Brooke is picking up the knick knacks that were knocked down but not broken, and Annabelle is sweeping the broken remnants of the lamp into a pile.

I know the bride and groom aren't supposed to see each other before the wedding, but Annabelle has never been a superstitious kind of girl. I bet she hates that decision right now, seeing as she is cleaning up her living room floor. I remember her and Conner getting into arguments about this. Him telling her that they are supposed to be away from each other the day of the wedding, followed by her yelling at him, saying they live together and have been together for years, so make her.

Once I hit the bottom step I start to look around, remembering my keys were on the front table last night. They have been since I arrived. Now there is just a big mess everywhere.

"Has anyone seen my keys? I need to go get the flowers," I announce to the room. I see lots of heads shake back and forth before Jackson speaks up, "Take my truck. Your Jetta has a spare on it anyway, so you shouldn't be driving it."

Realizing I don't have a better plan at the moment and still lack keys, I nod in agreement.

Reaching in the back pocket of his faded blue jeans, he pulls out his truck keys, tossing them to me.

Catching them, I hear him say, "It's the Toyota out front. Be easy on her, she can be stubborn."

Caught off guard by his comment, I look up at him to see him smiling. Then he winks at me before getting back to picking up wood fragments off the floor. Confused by his statement, I walk out the front door. She can be stubborn. Is he talking about me or his truck? Clearly trucks can't really be stubborn right?

I see his red Toyota pickup truck sitting beside Brooke's silver Nissan Rogue. Walking to it, I notice right away it is a man's truck. It is a king cab, but it's the big mud tires that drawl my attention. That, and the classic chrome rims along with the chrome step bar. Unlocking the door I begin to climb inside, finding that it is a workout. Why must his truck be so big? Thankfully I am wearing shorts or else I would've flashed my backside to everyone if I was in a skirt.

Once I am behind the wheel, I suddenly understand the reason for the big truck. I tower over everything. It's amazing! Looking down, I notice that it is a stick shift. *Great!* I haven't driven a stick shift since I learned how to drive. This should be fun! It's like riding a bike right? Starting the truck, the music comes blaring thru playing Kenny Loggins` "Danger Zone". I smile to myself, because I find that this song is so appropriate right now. Looking around to make sure no one is watching, I attempt to back out. After staling three times, I accomplish my goal. Thankfully by the time I get to the main road, I have just about got it figured out. Riding a bike my ass, I need some training wheels.

# Chapter 19

## *Did he hear me*

I get to the flower shop in one piece thankfully. As far as his truck goes, it might need a new clutch by the time I am done with it. Thinking I was only going to be grabbing a few flowers at the shop was an understatement. The flower guy and I spend almost thirty minutes loading up Jackson's truck full of bouquets, petals, and single roses. By the time we are done, his truck looks like a valley. That, or I have robbed the flower shop. I can't picture how Annabelle simply needs all these flowers for one event.

On the way home I listen to one of his old cd`s, Tim McGraw`s "Just To See You Smile". I have always loved that song. It makes me think of Jackson when I first met him. We used to play fight with each other all the time. I don't know what he gained out of it, but I know what I did. His body pressed up against mine and his arms wrapped around me in one way or another. I guess you could consider it my foreplay. Pulling into the drive way, Joe Nichols` "Tequila Makes Her Clothes Fall Off" comes on. I chuckle to myself, thinking this song was made about me.

Hoping out of the truck, I grab a handful of red roses and make my way inside, finding the place is cleaned up. Besides missing furniture, there are no dead giveaways about what happened last night. Walking into the kitchen, I set down Jackson`s keys on the island, when I see Brooke barreling through the back door.

"Great to have you back, girl. Do you need help unloading?" She asks.

"Yes, I think Annabelle bought out the whole flower shop," I say dramatically.

"I will unload, so you can go ahead and get started on the cakes. I know once that is done, Bridezilla might take it down a notch."

Smiling I reply, "Sure," before heading to the counter where the cakes are located.

I start clipping off the stems of the red roses in order to place them on top of the fondant. It takes me about an hour to completely finish the wedding cake. It is a three tiered cake with layers of red roses on the top of each tier. I place a red rose on each side of the cake at the bottom, to give it a final touch. It looks like something out of a magazine. I know Annabelle will love it. After I clean up my mess, I place the cake on the island. Admiring my work, I don't hear Jackson come up behind me until I feel the warmth of his body radiating on my back. He wraps one arm around my middle and uses the other one to sweep my pony tail off my neck. Kissing my neck, he whispers softly in my ear, "Looks beautiful babe."

I mutter, "Thanks," while turning around in his arms. Lifting my hands to his hair, I tilt my head to the side, pressing my lips to his. Wrapping his other arm around me, he pulls me up against him. I take the kiss deeper opening up my mouth, and his tongue sweeps inside mine. *God, he is a great kisser.* Seeking maximum contact, I press my chest to his. Lips together and tongues tangled, we continue kissing for a while. Then he moves his hands down my body, cupping my ass. Lifting me up, he places me on the counter. I spread my legs, so he can move further in between them. Using his arms, he pulls me closer to him, all the while never breaking our kiss. I wrap my legs around his hips and melt into him. He feels so good, and I wonder if I can convince him to take me now on the counter. Dropping my hands from his head, I make my way to the bottom of his shirt and start to pull it off. Tearing his lips away from mine, he growls, "I can't wait to be inside of you."

Opening my eyes I blurt, "Me neither." What the hell are we waiting for, is what I want to know?

Dropping his hands, he steps away from me and toward the fridge, "I was coming in here to grab a drink, but I just couldn't help myself when I saw you." Smiling I respond, "I just thought you had some kind of radar for me, because every time I come into the kitchen you seem to be close behind."

Jerking his head toward the window, I watch the sides of his mouth raise, "No radar, but a kitchen window babe." Opening up the fridge, he grabs a water bottle and takes a swig. "I was outside setting up for the wedding and saw you in the window. Just like all the other times, I couldn't help myself; I had to find an excuse to come inside."

"Ah, that explains it." Deciding that is my cue to leave, I walk over to him and press my hand on his chest. Leaning up on my tip toes, I whisper in his ear.

"I'm going to go grab a long hot shower, too bad you can't join me."

Muttering under his breath he says, "You are killing me. Now I have to walk outside with a hard on and try to help set up, all the while thinking of you naked in the shower."

Smiling at him, I walk out of the kitchen.

Making my way upstairs, I grab my shower bag and head off to the bathroom. Thinking I might just get lucky with Jackson, I decide to take my time and shave all the necessary areas. There is nothing worse than having him go down on you to find prickly legs and a bush that makes you think of the American pie movie. Flashing back to this morning, I remember his mouth on me and his hands on my breasts. I start to feel the ache between my legs when suddenly I have a fabulous idea. I am tired of being cut off short because of people interrupting us or him having good morals. I decide in that moment, I will take care of myself. It has been a while since I have masturbated, several months to be exact. Don't even get me started about the last guy I slept with. If he didn't go down on me, I didn't get off. Needless to say, my vibrator, named Bubba, has been my significant other for the last year. Moving my left hand to my breast, I tweak my nipple while my right hand goes in between my legs, honing in on my clit. With the mental image of Jackson coming out of the shower and what he did to me this morning, it didn't take but a few rolls of the clit and I was tossing my head back, biting my lip to stifle my moans.  Feeling satisfied, I finish up in the shower and hop out.

After putting on my lotion, I wrap the towel around me and grab my stuff. Walking out of the bathroom, I see Conner leaning up against the wall. He has his head down shaking it back and forth.

"Emily, Emily, Emily," he says, looking up at me with a huge smile on his face.

"Yes," I reply not understanding. To say I'm confused is an understatement. Did I do something that he finds amusing, that I don't remember?

"Please tell me I did not just hear what I think I did."

*Oh Shit!* My mouth drops open. You don't think he did, did he? I mean, I am loud but I figured with the shower it might drown it out.  Standing in my towel, I feel the blush hit my cheeks.

"I will take that as a yes," he says chuckling.

"Oh God, please don't tell anyone!" I beg.

With a huge smile he says, "Oh sweetie," putting his finger to his mouth, he taps it lightly. "I will try my best to keep my mouth shut, but I suggest you use Jackson next time. If I was him, I would be a little pissed if I found out my woman was taking care of herself."

"I'm not his woman!" I snap. I would like to be but we haven't discussed anything, so to be honest I don't know where we stand.

"You are," he states, before walking downstairs.

"UGH!" Making my way into my room, I shut the door. That has got to be the most embarrassing thing ever. I don't know how it would be for someone to catch you mid act, but listening to you do it to yourself has got to be right up there.

# Chapter 20

## *Try to tell me no now*

Ignoring what just happened, I get ready for the spa. I know they recommend wearing button up shirts when they are doing your hair, but I don't have any clean ones. So, I put on a bright yellow low cut, scoop neck tank top. It should be easy to get on and off without messing anything up. I add my yellow flip flops, since I will be getting a pedicure, and a pair of low riding faded blue jean shorts. I brush my hair and decide to let it air dry. They can tame the madness that becomes of it, once I get to the spa. Grabbing my purse, I head downstairs to find Brooke waiting patiently on the living room couch.

"All set," I say getting her attention.

"That's good, now we just have to pry Annabelle from outside," she says shaking her head.

Smiling, I tease, "Maybe if we get in the car and threaten to leave without her, she might get the hint and high tail it to the car."

Standing up, Brooke grabs her purse, "I am willing to try anything at this point."

Making our way out the front door to her Silver Nissan Rogue, Brooke shouts at Annabelle in the backyard.

"Get your ass in gear Annabelle or we are leaving without you."

Laughing I hop into the backseat of Brooke's car and watch Annabelle run across the yard toward us.

"You wouldn't dare, I'm the bride!" She says stunned.

"Try us," Brooke warns.

Obviously not willing to risk it, Annabelle plops her butt in the car.

Once we get down the road Annabelle turns around to face me, "So, have you and Jackson, ya know, bow chicka wow wow?"

*Way to break the ice.*

"That is none of your business," I reply innocently.

"I`m going to take that as a no," Brooke says.

Annabelle nods her head, "You made it my business last night when you told me he wouldn't."

"Wouldn't or couldn't? Like he has a problem? Because, I don't picture him having a problem. I have glanced down there on several occasions and it seems to be functioning properly," Brooke says, waving her finger in her private area for clarification purposes.

Sitting back in my seat, I shake my head back and forth and let them discuss it. No sense in opening my mouth. I am more than sure Annabelle is going to inform her of everything.

"Wouldn't," Annabelle says with a smile. "He wanted to make sure she wasn't drunk and would remember everything."

"How could you not remember? That man is built like a God!" Brooke blurts.

"That he is," Annabelle confirms. "So getting back to my question Emily, quit the bullshit and answer."

Shaking my head back and forth I confirm sadly, "No."

"Why," Annabelle asks?

"Yeah why? I would've locked him in a room already by now and had my way with him if I was you!" Brooke questions.

"We almost did this morning, I mean he was down there and everything," I say pointing to the apex of my thighs. "But then some high pitched Bridezilla came banging on the door and ruined everything."

Brooke bites her lip to stop from laughing out loud.

"You could've said something like, HEY! About to get some, back off!" Annabelle snaps.

Waving my hand in the air, I reply, "It's over and done, nothing to do about it now."

"You could drag him in a room and go at it like rabbits. Then come and give specific details to us later," Brooke remarks.

"You guys are perverts," I say, rolling my eyes.

"Yeah," they both agree simultaneously.

We arrive at the spa not long after we finish the conversation about Jackson and I doing the business, or in this case, lack thereof. It is a beautiful white brick building situated next to a coffee shop. Checking in at the front desk, they usher us down a hallway to the locker room where they hand us each a white plush robe. After we change, we are escorted to the main room. Looking around, I take it all in. On the far right wall is several hair styling stations. The back wall consist of closed off doors, where I am told they do waxing. The left side of the wall has multiple pedicure stations, and in the middle of the room are back to back nail stations. What I notice immediately is that there are no TV`s. The staff `divide and conquer`. A girl named Bridget takes Brooke to do her feet, while a lady named Trisha takes Annabelle to do her hair. I am given a nice woman named Jeanine, who walks me to her nail station. We take turns at each station, before we are done.

Walking out of the salon, we are equipped with French Manicure tips on our finger nails and toes, along with an up do for the wedding. My hair looks similar to Annabelle's and Brooke's. It is an upside down twist with spiral curls flowing out the top. There is just something about spa`s that are so relaxing and make you feel pretty. Riding on our happy high, we ride in silence back to the house.

Once we arrive, Annabelle scurries up to our room. She grabs all the things that she will need in order to get ready. Once she has everything, she takes it into Brooke's bathroom which has been designated the girls dressing room for the day. We have been told the men are going to be utilizing the hall bath to get ready. Grabbing my dress out of Brooke's room, I head to my bedroom. Since I don't wear much makeup, putting it on in the bedroom has never been a problem for me. Once I have my makeup completed, I get undressed. Unfortunately, with the dress being backless a bra is out of question. Good thing I still remain pretty perky these days. Since `no bra` doesn't scream sexy to me, I make a decision to go bold. Nothing ventured, nothing gained right? Taking a deep breath, I muster up all the courage I can and run through my reasons for my preposterous decision. First, my dress is floor length. It does have a slit on the right thigh, but it isn't that high. Second, just in case I get lost in the heat of the moment with Jackson, I don't want any barriers in my way. Third, if what my friends say is true, men find women going commando, irresistible and hot. Nodding my head to myself in the mirror as if accepting my reasoning, I pull off my panties and decide to go panty less. *Try to tell me no now Jackson.*

Grabbing my dress I slip it on. It is a satin black halter dress. There is a V at the front that starts on each side of the neck, and drops to a low point in between my breasts. It is floor length and has one slit up the right side to mid-thigh level. The back has the one piece of fabric at the neck, then nothing until

pg. 197

right above the butt. It is simple, elegant and shows off all of my curves in all the right areas. Putting on my black heels and diamond stud earrings, I take one last look in the mirror. Touching up my lipstick, I walk out my bedroom door.

# Chapter 21

## *So I can have a glass*


Knowing Annabelle was taken care of since her mom was upstairs helping and with Brooke being the maid of honor and assisting, I make my way downstairs. Walking down the steps, I see tons of people mingling around the house. I spot Jackson in the far corner of the living room. His hips are to the wall, with his hands in his suit jacket pockets and his feet are crossed at the ankle. He looks unbelievably handsome. As if sensing me, he looks up and winks. Smiling at him, I continue down the stairs.

He tips his head and says something to the older gentleman that he is talking with, before striding my way. Stopping at the bottom of the stairs, I wait for him to reach me. Tipping my head back, I look up into his eyes. He places one of his hands to my waist while bending his head, whispering in my ear, "You look absolutely stunning babe."

"Not so bad yourself, handsome."

Leaning his head back, he plants a quick kiss on my lips.

From across the room I hear, "Emily is that you?"

Not knowing where it`s coming from, I start looking around immediately.

Jackson stands upright, but moves to stand next to me. Sliding his hand at my waist further around my back,

I hear him mutter under his breath, "Jesus!"

Turning to look up at him, I see him leaning back, looking at the back of my dress.

"I think you are missing half of your dress babe," he growls.

"No I'm not, that's how it's made," I say smiling sweetly at him.

I notice out of the corner of my eye an older man coming toward me. Ah, he must be who called my name. Looking at him closely, I see that it is Annabelle's father.

"Mr. Hendricks it is so nice to see you," I say politely, leaning in for a hug.

"I thought that was you Emily. Gosh, you sure did grow up to be an exceptionally beautiful young lady didn't you. How have you been darling?"

"I'm wonderful, thank you. And you?"

"My daughter is getting married, so of course I'm doing well. Who is this young man with you?" He says pointing to Jackson.

*Oh!* How do I answer this? He's not with me, even though I want him to be and his arm is technically around my waist. How about, oh don't you remember? He is the guy that I have been completely in love with for my entire life. Deciding against that, I go for casual and indirect.

"This is Jackson Calright. We knew each other when Annabelle and I were in high school."

"Mr. Hendricks," Jackson says putting out his hand.

Taking it, they shake hands while Mr. Hendricks studies him.

"It is so nice that our Emily has finally settled down. What is it that you do for a living Jackson?"

*Oh no!* How do I stop this? I don't want to be rude and correct Annabelle's father, but I don't want to mislead him either. Worse, I don't know if this potential thing will scare off Jackson. Quickly I say, "Oh um, Mr. Hendricks we aren't…." when Jackson cuts me off. Talking over me Jackson says, "I am happy to have her as well Mr. Hendricks. As far as my work, I am an FBI agent up in D.C."

*WHAT?* He lives close to me and I didn't even know it? Wait, he is in the FBI? That's HOT! Agent Calright. *Sweet Mercy!* I really love the sound of that.

Turning my head toward Jackson with my mouth wide open, I am about to blurt are you kidding me! But then I feel his fingers at my back dig in, while he shoots me a look that unmistakably says *shut your mouth, we will discuss this later*. Deciding not to cross him, I clamp my mouth shut and turn my head back to

Mr. Hendricks, plastering a smile on my face.

"That's amazing," Mr. Hendricks says, "Takes a lot of kahunas to do that. Well I will leave you guys to it. I`m going to go grab another beer while I can."

Thinking that sounds like a fabulous idea, I turn and look back at Jackson once Mr. Hendricks has walked off. "Before we discuss you being an FBI agent and living close to me, I want to know the ground rules for this drinking thing. Say I want to have a glass of champagne or two with the toast, is that going to make you deny me later?"

"Babe."

Waving at him to hush it, I finish, "I`m not done. I don't know about you, but it is an open bar and I could use a drink. Also it might help with our conversation for later about well… everything. Another reason is I need the liquid courage for walking down the aisle in front of everyone. So, how much is too much before you cut me off?"

I know I might sound pathetic right now, but I don't care. I want him, but I also want a drink to calm my nerves. Smiling he responds, "Babe, that's not going to happen."

Incredibly confused I state, "But you said the other night you wouldn't sleep with me, because I was drinking or possibly drunk."

"That was then. Now that I know you want me as much as I want you, there will be no stopping this."

*Oh!* I like the sound of that. But wanting to clarify just to make sure I don't fuck this up and manage not to get fucked literally, I ask, "So, I can drink however much I want and you and I will still… ya know…"

Leaning into me, "You are standing in what I consider half a dress. No, there is no stopping this. If you want I can take you upstairs and put your fears at ease," he says winking at me.

"Not that that doesn't sound awesome, but we don't have time and I would mess up my hair." God, now I am the one making excuses.

"That's what I thought. But, if I may suggest, just knowing you, maybe don't drink too many before you walk down the aisle. We both know how clumsy you are."

"Good point. I will stick with one glass then," I say smiling, "Shall we?"

"After you," he says motioning toward the kitchen.

If he thinks this is half a dress, what is he going to say when he finds out that I don't have anything on underneath it? Oh, that is going to be fun. But I will wait until later to torment him.

Making our way into the kitchen, I try to focus on everything but his hand on my back. The skin to skin contact is making me ache between the legs with anticipation for later. I am starting to rethink my decision about going up stairs for a quickie, when I see a hand reach out toward Jackson's arm. Looking over I see that it is Savannah. *Ugh! That bitch!*

"Jackson I have been looking everywhere for you." Savannah says smiling at him, batting her eyes. *God!*

This is unpleasant. Pulling my lips together, I decide it is best to make a quick getaway, toward the alcohol of course.

"I am going to be over....there," I say motioning to the side of me, "Bye."

With that I walk away as quick as my heels can take me without tripping.

Oh dear lord, what if I do fall. If I trip and my dress pulls to far on one side, I could pop a boob out. Or if my dress comes up, they might see my lady parts. *Oh sweet mercy.* I need to rethink my decision on going commando.

The open bar isn't until the reception. As for right now, they have several different kinds of beer bottles in coolers on the floor with a selection of different wines on the counter. Making my way toward the wine, I grab a glass and fill it to the rim. I wish they had the ones here like out of Cougar town that can fit a whole bottle in one glass. It won't help me walk down the aisle, but it will make me feel better about being around Savannah all night.

Turning around I see Jackson glaring at me. That can't be good. If I didn't know better, I would say he is pissed off at me. Taking a sip I watch him as he limits the distance between us. "Why did you walk off?" He clips.

Yep, he`s pissed.

"She seemed eager to talk to you," I reply annoyingly.

"I don't care; I don't want to talk to her," he snaps.

Pulling my lips together, I choose not to push it.

Instead I decide to change the subject, "You work for the FBI?"

"Yes," he says directly.

"When did you get out of the military?" I push him, wanting to know more.

"After I did my four years," he says deadpan.

Guessing he doesn't want to talk about it due to his very short responses, I change it up.

"I didn't know you worked so close to me. I live in Alexandria."

"I know," he responds firmly.

*What?* You do. How? Maybe Annabelle told him, but why would she?
Looking me in the eyes, he confesses, "I kept track of you."

I am speechless. I want to ask why, but I can't seem to form words. Instead I find myself just staring at him. I know how he did it; his job obviously gave him that advantage. I also know that him keeping track of me is stalker like and should be considered creepy. I should even be appalled, but I'm not. Instead I find it sweet, endearing and tremendously arousing. What is wrong with me? If any other person said this to me, I would've slapped them. I probably would've even gotten a restraining order. But seeing that I have been in love with him all my life, I'm glad. Maybe that means he does like me.
Concerned, he asks, "Are you mad?"
"No," I answer truthfully, finishing off my glass of wine.

Before I can say anything else an announcement is made that it is time for everyone to take their seats, so the ceremony can begin. Setting my glass down, I make my way across the kitchen in search of Brooke.

# Chapter 22

## *Karma is a bitch*

Walking to the bottom of the stairs, I see Brooke heading toward me. "Once everyone gets situated we will go ahead and start things," she says looking down the hall, toward the back door.

I use this time to take it all in. Right outside the back door and to the right is a white oak table. On the table is a bouquet of white flowers, with a guest sign in sheet under it. Looking straight ahead, there is a red and white rose petal walkway with white folding chairs set up in rows on each side. There looks to be about fifty seats total. Centered in front of the chairs, is the wedding arch. It has a white flower bouquet at the top, with two little ones on each side. The arch is intertwined with different greens and baby's breath in the middle that extends to the bottom. White tulle stretches from the top of the arch, out to the sides before falling to the ground. At the bottom of the arch are two huge bouquets of red roses and white tulips, setting in white flower pots. On each side of the arch, where the wedding party stands, is a pole with red roses and white tulips at the top. It is small, simple and exquisite.

After about ten minutes of waiting, the preacher gives the nod, letting us know that it is time to begin. Ready to walk out, I turn around and notice Annabelle approaching. My mouth drops open when I see her in her wedding dress. She stops walking and spins slowly to give us all a view. It is a full length Ivory off the shoulder, trumpet gown with Chantilly lace flower details etched all over, complete with a small train. The middle of the back to where the front shoulder straps connect, is a see thru lace material. She decided to go with a small floral inspired rhinestone hair clip, instead of a veil or tiara. She completes the dress with a crystal stretch link bracelet borrowed from her mother, pairing it with her old diamond teardrop crystal earrings. She finished off the something old, new, borrowed and blue, with a blue accented garter. She is truly the most beautiful bride I have ever seen.

Hearing the music start to play "Canon in D", I know it is my cue. Grabbing my red and white bouquet, I turn around walking out the back door. I thought I would be nervous, but come to find out I wasn't. Looking around, I notice Jackson at the front standing next to Nathan. With a smile on my face, I lock eyes with him and continue down the aisle. Assuming my position in the bridesmaid spot, I turn around and focus on Brooke walking down the aisle. Hearing the music change to "Here Comes the Bride", I watch Annabelle glide thru the back door towards us.

During the service, I can't help but sneak peeks at Jackson. Every time I do, it seems as if he senses me staring at him and glances up at me. We smile, he winks and I blush like a schoolgirl because I was just caught staring and immediately look away. We do this numerous times until I hear the preacher doing the exchanging of the rings. I always loved this part of the ceremony. To look up and see the love in each of their eyes makes me tear up every time. I want that someday. To find someone who will love me unconditionally like that. To get married, have a family and grow old together. *One day.*

After they announce the new Mr. and Mrs. LeBlanc, they walk hand and hand down the aisle to the "Wedding March". Following behind them are Brooke and Nathan. It dawns on me then, I will be walking down the aisle with Jackson. We might be going the wrong way and not actually getting married, but this is as close as I am going to get. *Karma is a bitch!* Jackson strides over to me and I wrap my arm in his as we proceed to walk down the aisle.

We don't speak much after the ceremony during the picture taking process. We exchange glances and smile, but mostly keep to ourselves. I blame the photographer on it. She might be awesome at taking pictures but when directing people where to stand, she is more like a drill sergeant. At one point, I could've sworn when Jackson walks by me, his fingertips trailed lightly along my back. I didn't think it happened at first, until I noticed the goose bumps that were left from his touch.

What seemed like forever only turned out to be twenty minutes of endless picture taking. Annabelle was right though, the sun setting in the back ground will make for beautiful pictures. Once the wedding party, besides the bride and groom, were done taking pictures, we made our way to the barn for the reception.

# Chapter 23

## *He's right*


    Walking into the barn, I notice the set up and stop immediately to take it all in. The hoedown was beautiful, but looking at this place now is like looking at a magazine. The ceiling is lined with lights that are hanging off of a string that stretches from the middle of the room, out to all different sides. Creating a beautiful glow around the entire room. Occasionally you will see the white round decorative lantern lights hanging from the wire, accenting the other lights. At the door and to the right is a table with a white table cloth on it that is smothered in gifts. Down the wall from the gift table is where the bar is located. In the corner on the left side of the barn, across from the gift table is where the DJ is set up. Further along that wall is where the cake table is situated. *God, the cake looks gorgeous*. The dance floor is centered in the middle of the room. At the back of the barn are individual round tables with chairs circling them. The tables are covered in white table cloths with red rose petals scattered on top of them. Each table is set up with a tiny bouquet of white flowers in a clear vase with tea lights circling them.

Between the round tables, is a small rectangular table. This is the bride and groom's table, which is also covered in a white table cloth with red rose petals scattered along the top. It has a crystal looking candle holder as the centerpiece, followed by two small bouquets of white flowers in clear vases sitting on the edge of the table. Most people would say it is weird that Annabelle chose red and white for her decorations, but accented by the natural colors of the barn, it works well.

Standing in awe at my surroundings, I don't notice who passes by me and who doesn't. It's not until I feel Jackson's arm curve around my back, that I realize he has been standing next to me the entire time.

"You guys did an amazing job. It`s breathtakingly beautiful," I say in awe. "I am impressed myself. It helped that Annabelle gave Conner a picture diagram with specific instructions of what she wanted and where. Not to mention, Conner wanting to make sure it was perfect for his bride on her wedding day."

"She will love it." I say turning my head to look up at him. "I know, because I do."

"How about we go find our table?" He says gesturing with his free hand.

Making our way to the end of the dance floor, we find the bridal party table. It is just to the right of the bride and groom`s table. I smile to myself thinking how convenient it is that we are sitting next to each other. If I didn't know better, I would start to think Annabelle and Conner had planned this from the beginning.

Sitting down, the waitress comes over and ask what we want to drink. I`m impressed that Annabelle went to such lengths to have the wedding catered with plated meals and a wait staff. I remember that conversation on the phone where she and Conner got into a heated battle. She said she would give up a destination wedding or a wedding at a church, but she refused to have a buffet or a pot luck event. If it was going to be at her parent's old farm house, then she was going all out. And she did.

The staff brings our drinks, and I take a hefty sip right away.

"You okay," He asks.

"Yeah. Why?" I ask curiously.

"Just wondering if your downing the wine as if its water in the desert because of the wedding, me or for our impending conversation later."

Not knowing exactly what to say, I shrug my shoulders and decide not to lie.

"A little bit of all of it I guess."

He nods, taking a swig of his beer.

"Care to elaborate?" He asks curiously.

"Not really," I reply glancing around the room.

"Later then," he says in a firm tone.

Nodding in agreement, I look the other way immediately.

Thankfully conversation is ceased with the introductions of Mr. and Mrs. LeBlanc's arrival. Making their way across the room, an announcement is made that dinner will start being served.

That's good, because I am starved and need something to start soaking up all the alcohol. I can tell I am already starting to get a buzz. While we wait, we make conversation with family and friends that stop by the table.

Dinner is served not long after, and it looks scrumptious. Digging in, I try to ignore the fact that Jackson's leg is pushed up against mine. When his hand moves and rest on my leg, my whole body jolts. He slowly moves his fingers to push open the slit on my dress, touching me skin to skin, sending a shiver thru my body. Looking around to see if anybody noticed, I see the corner of Jackson's lips go up. *Shit he did.* As if that was the seal of approval, he inches his hand further up my leg causing my dress to ride up. Crossing my legs, I clamp them shut at the same time my hand goes under the table to stop him.

Between the wine and his hands on me, it is becoming painful to be this close to him. Especially, when I am fully aware of what may happen later. Looking over at him, I take him all in.

He has taken off his suit jacket and undone the collar of his shirt. Leaving his top two buttons undone, exposing a tiny glimpse of his chest. Looking up I see he has shaved this morning and his face is stubble free. Not to mention his chiseled jaw, smooth, full delicious lips, and piercing blue eyes. His hair looks like he has run his hands through it several times. Taking in a breath, the scent of his cologne hits my nose. I really do love that smell. I look up at him to see he is staring at me, but not at my eyes. He is staring at my lips. Deciding I want to feel them again, I lick my lips and lean in toward him. I'm about to shut my eyes, when I hear the DJ on the microphone call the first dance.

Jumping back in my seat, I watch Annabelle and Conner get up and move to the middle of the room. They dance gracefully to "At last" by Etta James. When they are done, the DJ announces open floor and the music changes.

Leaning over toward me Jackson asks, "May I have this dance?"

Placing my hand in his, we start walking to the dance floor. Once we hit the middle of the floor, he pulls me into his arms and we slow dance to "Making Memories of Us" by Keith Urban. When the song changes to "Gorilla" by Bruno Mars, he pulls back and spins me. I get in one spin, until I realize OH SHIT! I need to stop. I can feel my dress moving at the top. Afraid I will flash everyone, I clamp my body to Jackson's. He tenses for a brief second caught off guard by my sudden movement, but accepts me. Tilting his head down he asks, "You okay?"

"Yeah, I just…" *Crap!* What do I say? "I just need to um… sit down," I say hesitantly.

"Are you sick?" He asks worriedly.

"No," I blurt. After looking around briefly, I peak down at my chest to make sure I'm all good. I am. *Thank god.*

Looking up at him, I see he followed my eyes down to my chest. I give him a couple seconds then watch his eyes slide back up to mine.

Eyebrows raised he pushes, "You sure you`re okay?"

Since I'm a crap liar and can't think on my feet, I decide this is the perfect time to start torturing him.

"Yeah, just um… this dress isn't conducive for a bra and I don't want anything to fall out." I say slightly embarrassed.

His eyes flash, before he leans down further to me, "You're not wearing a bra? I guess you really can't since its missing a back, huh?"

"Nope. Just a dress and heels. That's it," I clarify.

His arms tense around me, "Wait, are you not wearing…" He stops talking, but I feel his hands spray a little lower as if checking for my panty line. "Jesus. Tell me you are shitting me!"

"Nope," I reply sweetly.

"I have got to see this!"

Releasing one hand from around my waist, he uses the other to lead me off the dance floor.

Guiding me out of the barn doors and to the side of the building, he pushes me back until I am pinned up against the wall by his body. My breath catches and I find myself instantly aroused. Grabbing both of my hands, he pulls them up above my head. Using his left hand he holds my wrists together. Taking his right hand, he slowly skims it down my arms. His head dips down and starts trailing kisses from my ear, down around my neck, while his hand continues sliding down my body and over my breasts, making my nipples harden. Then his hand sinks further down my belly past my hip and continues to my thigh, until it meets the slit of my dress. Panting, he raises his head and kisses me on the lips passionately. Placing his hand inside the slit of my dress, I feel his fingertips brush my thigh as they make their way up to the sensitive lips of my sex. *Sweet Jesus!*

Breaking the kiss he whispers in my ear, "Is this all for me?" As he slides his finger up and down my aching flesh, spreading my juices all over me. His thumb finds my clit and rolls, causing me to moan out loud. Doing another delicious twirl with his thumb, he attempts to muffle my moans, by kissing me roughly. We are so lost in the moment we don't realize Conner walks by until he speaks.

Clearing his throat, Conner smiles saying, "My bad, didn't mean to interrupt you guys. Glad to see you took my advice though Emily in deciding to use Jackson." With that, he walks off. Jackson tenses before stepping back, releasing my hands from over my head. My eyes instantly hit his, to see they are guarded.

"What the fuck did he mean, deciding to use me?" He says in a hard firm tone that can only be taken as `don't fuck with me.`

*God!* That must be his FBI take charge voice. Why do I find it hot?

"I…" I stammer, unable to form words. I look around as if the answer will come to me.

"Are you playing me?" He snaps.

"No," My eyes shoot to him, pleading.

His jaw muscles jump, "Explain then NOW!"

"Okay… You see Conner over heard me…" *Oh God!* This is embarrassing.

His eyes flash, "KEEP GOING EMILY!" He says angrily.

Oh boy, I`m back to Emily, not babe. He must be really pissed off at me.

"He heard me in the shower finishing myself off after you left me high and dry this morning. He said that I was your woman and I should use you for that. That if it was him, he would be pissed that I was… ya know… to myself," I blurt quickly.

He stands there for a second, I assume letting it sink in that I was indeed masturbating earlier in the shower. *Geez!*

"He's right," he clarifies.

*What?* He is. "He's right?" I say confused.

"Yeah"

"He is?" I say still confused. Looking up into his eyes, I see the anger is gone. Stepping into me, his right hand comes up behind my head bringing it toward him, crushing his lips to mine in a hungry way. My hands fist in his hair, as I melt into his kiss.

Pulling his lips away, he leans his forehead to mine. I watch his lips curve up into a smile as I feel my heart skip a beat.

"Let's get out of here. I believe I owe you something," he says softly.

"Thank god!" I say relieved.

# Chapter 24

## *Let`s Go*

    As we start walking toward the house I hear an annoying voice screech, "EMILY!"

"Shit!" Jackson growls, readjusting himself.

*Failed again!* This is becoming the story of my life.

From the barn we hear, "Has anyone seen Emily?"

The sound we hear is Annabelle on a microphone. Who in their right mind would freely hand over a microphone to Annabelle?

Sighing, we make our way into the barn. "There she is. Everyone before we cut this fabulous cake, I want to give a shout out to Emily for making it for me last minute. Come on over here girl."

Making my way over to the cake, Jackson separates from me and heads to the bar. Can't blame him, I want a drink too!

I see Conner beside Annabelle with his head down and shoulders going up and down. That douche is laughing. He knows what she interrupted and he finds it amusing. Crap, he interrupted us right before she did. It was probably his idea. *UGH!*

"I just wanted to say thank you and tell everyone where this fabulous cake came from," Annabelle explains.

"Thanks, but it's not necessary. Let's just eat it already," I respond smiling, before stepping back.

After the traditional cake cutting part of the ceremony, they turn the music back on. Hearing that it is Pitbull and Keisha singing "Timber", I drag Brooke who's next to me to the dance floor. I know my dress is an issue, so I decide to hold it with my hands. Once we get out onto the dance floor, Annabelle joins us and we cut loose like if we are the only three people in the room. I keep looking over to Jackson during the song, who's at the bar with Nathan. I liked that every time I looked over, his eyes were always on me. I was trying my best to flirt with him while out on the dance floor by raising my eyebrows up and down several times, doing provocative moves with my hands, even licking my lips. When I see him approaching me, I couldn't help the huge grin on my face, I knew I had accomplished my goal.

The DJ switched up the music, for what I could only assume was to appease all members of the crowd. The song changed to "Boogie Shoes" by KC and the Sunshine Band. Thinking Jackson was going to just drag me off the dance floor, I was surprised when he spun me around and we started dancing. He is such a good dancer. Watching his hips move, sends a fire deep down in my belly. There isn't anything sexier than watching a man who can dance. When the song ended, he stated firmly, "Let's go."

Biting my lip, I do as he says, following him off the dance floor and out of the barn.

This is it! This is what I have been waiting for. *YAY!* Please God, no more interruptions.

When we get into the house, we go straight upstairs to my bedroom. Opening up the door, he waits for me to walk in before turning around and locking the door. Turning back to face me, he slowly stalks toward me unbuttoning his shirt. My heart begins beating faster and my breaths are coming quicker. Bending slightly, he picks me up catching me off guard and I gasp. Kicking off my shoes, he slowly lowers me to the bed, taking my mouth with what I can only describe as desperation. I slide one hand into his hair, the other hand going to his back, pulling him closer to me, with our tongues embracing each other in a rhythmic motion. Seeking as much contact as I can, I push his shirt off his shoulders, letting it fall to the floor before pressing my body into his. He breaks the kiss, but only to drag his teeth across my bottom lip making me moan. Sliding my hands over his bare chest, I reach down to start undoing his slacks. "No," he growls, pulling my hands away. Frustrated, I let out a whimper.

He smiles explaining, "This night is for you."

With that he reaches down with both hands and pulls my dress up and over my head.

Lowering himself to me, he begins kissing me. His lips are demanding, coaxing mine. Holding the majority of his body weight in his left arm, he hovers over me. He starts nibbling, kissing and dragging his lips from my ear down my chest. I can't help the shivers that run over my body. He stops at my left breasts, cupping it with his right hand. Lowering his head, he sucks on my right nipple while using his thumb and finger to roll my left one. I moan, feeling the sensation deep down. He tugs with his teeth on my right nipple while he pulls my left nipple hard. My hands dive into his hair and pull, making him groan. Running his tongue down my belly to my navel, he nips along the way until he reaches his destination. "Jackson," I plead breathlessly.

Using his left hand, he spreads my thighs wide, while his right hand moves between them. Sliding two fingers inside of me, he strokes me deep within. Then spreading my folds with his tongue, he licks my swollen clit, creating a continuous pattern that drives me insane. Then he pulls the tip of my folds into his mouth and sucks my bud, nipping it with his teeth. Gripping his hair tighter, my entire body tenses under him. I cry out in pleasure, drawing my thighs to his head, in order to hold him there until the orgasm subsides.

Standing up, he kicks off his shoes and then unzips his slacks, allowing them to fall to the floor with his boxers. Lowering himself back over me, he positions himself between my thighs with his arms on each side of my head, holding himself up. My hands move up his arms, over his tattoo and lock onto his biceps in preparation of him entering me. Locking eyes with him, I can feel him lining himself up to enter me. Bending his head, he kisses me deeply. "Please," I beg him, lifting up and biting his bottom lip causing him to groan.

In one swift movement he rocks into me, causing my head to fall back. I raise my hips and met him thrust for thrust as he pounds into me. Shifting his position, he goes deeper causing moans to escape my mouth. Dragging my hands down his body, I bite his shoulder to silence myself. I can feel it building again. Digging my nails into his bottom, I try to bring him deeper into me. As if sensing what I want, he starts going harder and faster. Then it washes over me. Throwing my head back, my back arches off the bed and I let go, shattering into pieces under him. He thrust into me several more times, before grounding out my name. Dropping his head to my forehead, we stay like this till our breaths slow down.

Pulling out slowly, he lies down beside me.

"Wow," he mutters.

"Yeah," I mumble still slightly breathless.

Twisting his head, he looks at me, "I didn't use protection."

"Don't worry, I'm on the pill." I assure him.

Propping up on one elbow, he pushes a piece of hair off my face before bending his head down and kissing me softly.

"You don't know how long I have wanted to do that with you babe."

"Probably as long as I have," I say chuckling.

Grinning he replies, "Yeah, you're probably right."

Laying back down, he pulls me into his arms. Settling my head on his chest, I wrap my arms around his waist. Hiking my leg up and over his, I snuggle into his warm body. While closing my eyes, I feel him kiss my head lightly. Listening to his breathing, I fall asleep effortlessly in his arms.

# Chapter 25

## *My Forever*

I am not a cuddlier. Typically I can't stand sharing my bed, so when I wake up to find myself wrapped around Jackson I am astounded. *Go figure!* I'm even drawn to him in my sleep.

Sensing that I am awake, I feel his fingers move over my stomach while he places feather light kisses on my neck. I turn around, until I come face to face with him. Kissing him gently, I run my hands down his chest. Placing my hand on his hard ridged length, I hear him growl. I move my body down his, stroking him as I go. Bending my head down, I wrap my lips around his shaft, taking him deep until I can feel him at the back of my throat. His hands reach down and fist my hair, holding me in place. Moving my head up and down, I suck his length. Stopping every once in a while to flick my tongue across his tip. His hips buck, while a moan escapes his mouth. I slide my tongue down his shaft, and then up before I wrap my lips around his head, restarting the process all over again.

Pulling my hair back, he mutters, "Ride me."

Doing as he says, I sit up and look down at his length as a shiver rolls over me in anticipation. Positioning myself over him, I plunge into him, releasing a hiss. His hands hold me in place at my hips. Tilting down I kiss him, his eagerness matching mine. I carefully rise up and lower myself back down, grinding into him. His hands slid up my waist, as if savoring the touch. I repeat the move over and over again. When I feel myself on the brink of release, I lift up but this time I crash down onto him, grinding hard. Rolling my hips against him again, I collapse onto his chest and let the orgasm rush through me. Flipping me over, he pounds into me several more times until he finds his own release, coming in a rush. Letting his body settle on mine, he pulls out and we lay there in silence.

After a while I know I need to get up and get dressed. The wedding festivities are over and it is time to go home. Do I just plain out ask him if this was an out of state thing, like what happens in Vegas stays in Vegas. *God!* I absolutely hate later conversations. Sitting up, I swing my feet to the side of the bed.

"Where are you going?" He asks.

Turning to look at him I state, "I am going to get dressed, then start packing."

"You aren't driving off on that spare tire of yours."

"What? Why not?" I ask confused.

"Because it says short distances, not twelve hours."

"Well then, I really need to get up. I need to locate an auto shop and get my tire fixed. Then I need to head home. But first, I need to find my keys."

"I have your keys," he clarifies.

"You do?" How does he have them? Maybe he found them.

"I have had them since I drove your car home after fixing your tire."

pg. 237

"You have? Why didn't you give them to me when I needed to go get the flowers?" I ask, still slightly confused.

"Because you aren't supposed to drive on a spare babe," he says.

I start to stand, when he places a hand on my shoulder.

"Are we going to talk about this?" He says motioning between us.

Biting my lip, I shrug my shoulders.

I really do want to have this conversation. But I don't want to go first, that's for sure. I laid my feelings out on the line and was rejected by him once, I know that my heart can't take that again.

"Well I know I do," he says curtly.

"Then why don't you go first," I suggest.

"Fine." Sliding his hand down my arm he grabs my hand, holding it in his. "I am not letting you slip out of my life again. We have wasted too much time as it is. I want this to work between us."

"You do?" I ask cautiously.

"Of course I do. You didn't think this was just a weekend fling, right?"

Shrugging my shoulders, I reply, "We never talked about it."

"Jesus, babe," he says, shaking his head back and forth. "That's why when you introduced me to Mr. Hendricks you were vague. And then, you tried to correct him when he said we were together," he states.

"I didn't want to assume anything," I explain.

"Well let me clear it up for you. I kept track of you because I wanted to see you, but I didn't know how to approach you. Seeing you walk through the front doors that first night you got here, I realized this was my chance. My chance to make up for turning you down all those years ago. I knew it was my chance to give you your forever."

"My forever," I whisper.

"Yeah babe, I remember you having conversations with Annabelle all those years ago about wanting to get married, have kids and grow old together. I want that with you," he explains.

"You heard me tell Annabelle that?" I clarify.

"Yeah."

"You want forever with me?" I ask hesitantly.

"Yeah, babe."

I couldn't believe my ears. Swallowing hard, I try to fight the lump in my throat. I was not going to cry or squeal.

"Let's get dressed and go find you a tire. We have a long road ahead of us," he says smiling.

Epilogue


*One year later*

"Told you I would give you your forever," Jackson whispers in my ear. Leaning up on my tip toes I give him a kiss, "Thank you."
"Would you two stop it, some of us are having problems keeping our food down watching you guys." Annabelle says.
"That's because you are pregnant. It has nothing to do with us," Jackson retorts.
Smiling sweetly I reply, "It's my wedding, I am allowed to molest him in public."
"Whatever," Annabelle says walking off.
I am so happy we decided to go with a red Empire gown for her. It allows plenty of room for her growing belly. Looking around the room I can't help but smile. Jackson has given me my forever.

I am standing in my Ivory strapless crinkle Chiffon gown with asymmetrical draping, and a crystal and pearl accented tiara. Annabelle has let me borrow her crystal teardrop earrings, and I have on my diamond tennis bracelet that Jackson gave me for our first Christmas. I top off the traditional something old, new, borrowed and blue, with a blue garter. Our actual ceremony today was on the beach. It was small and intimate, but decorated similar to Annabelle's wedding. Now standing at our reception, I think back to how it all began.

After we left Annabelle's wedding and got home, we started dating like a normal couple. It was convenient that his apartment lease was up in one month, causing us to move in together right away. It didn't really change things seeing how he was over every night anyway. He proposed three months into our relationship. Some people said we were rushing into things, but seeing how I had known him since I was fifteen, I didn't agree. Around the ninth month we bought a house together. It is a cute little four bedroom, two and a half bath, in a new development. "Perfect for a growing family," was what Jackson had said. We agreed to start trying to have children after the wedding, by going off the pill and letting nature do the rest. With him being able to pay the bills, I was able to quit working as a nurse. Allowing me to focus my attention on my dream of opening up my own bakery.

"You ready to head home babe?" Jackson says, pulling me into his arms, and out of my day dream.

"Yes."

"Good, I think we should go get a head start on making that family of ours Mrs. Calright," he says seductively.

"I like the sound of that. Do we need to say goodbye or tell anyone that we are leaving?" I ask.

"It's our wedding babe; we can do anything we want," he says, winking at me.

With a wave to Annabelle and Conner we sneak out the front door of the restaurant where we held the reception. Stepping out onto the curb, I turn around and look back at our guest enjoying themselves. Turning to look up at Jackson, I realize in that moment that I finally have what I have always wanted since I was a teenager, my forever with Jackson. Taking a deep breath, I look up to the stars and whisper, "Thank you."